HAUNTED TRAVELLER

HAUNTED TRAVELLER

An Imaginary Memoir

BARRY YOURGRAU

ARCADE PUBLISHING
NEW YORK

First Arcade Paperback Edition 2016

Parts of this book have previously appeared in *Story, Speak*, and *ArtCommotion*.

Arcade Publishing books may be purchased in bulk at special discounts for sales promotion, corporate gifts, fund-raising, or educational purposes. Special editions can also be created to specifications. For details, contact the Special Sales Department, Arcade Publishing, 307 West 36th Street, 11th Floor, New York, NY 10018 or arcade@skyhorsepublishing.com.

Arcade Publishing® is a registered trademark of Skyhorse Publishing, Inc.®, a Delaware corporation.

Visit our website at www.arcadepub.com.

10 9 8 7 6 5 4 3 2 1

Library of Congress Cataloging-in-Publication Data is available on file.

Cover design by Laura Klynstra

Print ISBN: 978-1-62872-700-5

Printed in the United States of America

TO *V. S.*

Those are the best journeys...at your own fireside...
SOMERSET MAUGHAM, "HONOLULU"

Perpetually in my imagination I could see the forests of
America, the jungles of Africa, the taiga of Siberia.
The words Orinoco, Mississippi and Sumatra
rang like music in my ears.
ALEXANDER GRIN, *COLLECTED WORKS*

When a man reaches a certain age, there are many things he
can simulate; happiness is not one of them.
JORGE LUIS BORGES, "SHAKESPEARE'S MEMORY"

CONTENTS

Gratitude and appreciation from the heart, for their patience, fortitude and generosity in the face of years (and years) of hauntedness...to Douglas Gayeton, Knight Landesman, Tom Schnabel. More of same to Juliet Bashore and Aaron Slavin, Virginia Hatley and Steve Swiatkiewics; to my brother Palle; and especially, as ever, Matt Lewis Thorne, and John Thorne.

An authorial salute to my exemplary editor, Coates Bateman, and to Sean McDonald. And to my indefatigable, innovative agent, Eileen Cope.

Seas & *INNS*
TROPICS & *Frontiers*
Northern Ghosts
Mountains & *PONIES*
Deserts, SNOWS & *Jungles*
HOTELS & *Monkeys*
& Crimes

HAUNTED TRAVELLER

Dialogue

DIALOGUE

Who are you?"

"A traveller."

"From where?"

"The place before this."

"Going where?"

"The place following."

"Ah, a conversationalist of a certain cryptic style, I see. Seeking what, if you please?"

"Whatever you care to name."

"It makes no matter, is that what you mean?"

"Whatever."

"But such an attitude, for having journeyed, doubtless, such great distances?"

"All distances are great."

"Surely not if I just cross the road."

"You quibble, and I'm not a philosopher. Though, lost in thought, I might traverse a whole world, pacing from one wall of my room to the other."

"Ah, then you're a kind of poet."

"And not, you think, a maniac?"

"Curious assurance, to be asking of a stranger!"

"And why not a stranger?"

"But we've scarcely met, I hardly know you!"

"A feeling I often share regarding myself. . . ."

"Now you descend, I'm afraid, into the true shallows of philosophical cliché."

"Yes, that's a hazard of travel: it promotes half-baked metaphysics. And an appetite for their expression."

"Surely not for all travellers!"

"Indeed. But now you see the kind of traveller you have before you."

FOG

Fog delays my plane en route. The aircraft sits on the dark mountain runway with its wing lights blinking, but its propeller is still and the fuselage door shut at the top of the mobile staircase. A woman passenger drinks the weak brandy at the dingy bar counter in the terminal hut. I pace up and down languidly, peering out through the mist-grimed windowpane. "This lousy weather," grumbles the woman at the bar. Her lavish hair is yoked with a dashing headband. "Oh, I don't mind it," I reply. "I'm a poet, you see. I'm writing a verse epic all about delays." The woman blinks at me and scowls, puzzled and disapproving. I grin. "Just a joke," I tell her. "I can't stand this either."

I drift over to a warm armchair and settle down, with that mix of tedium and anxiety particular to the circumstances. A while later the woman comes swaying over in my direction. She sinks into a neighboring chair in a glamorous heap, like a meteor expiring in a blaze of chic garments. Our pilot materializes behind her. He sits on her chair's armrest. He is seedily good-looking and rakish in his worn-out uniform. He strokes the woman's heedless shoulder. "Just as well she is like this," he observes. "In a fog of her own. . . . Such a beautiful lady is an angel of death," he declares. "She is bad luck to a journey by air." He grins at the look on my face. He winks. "Just a joke," he says.

The fog lifts a while later, and the plane takes off. When the woman awakens, I call for coffee and we hit it off. More bad weather forces us down again, but now on a lush coast. We decide to break off our journey altogether for now, and madly we lose a month to pleasure . . . in sun-bleached cheap hotels in the far corners of villages, in hammocks at twilight by the sands of a humid, isolated bay. Thanks to fog we lie entwined, letting the warm sea shove us about like flotsam.

But the woman is too fond of drink, and early one groggy morning, I sneak away to the local airport, alone.

My life resumes its interrupted course. Six months pass. One day I receive a letter. It's from her. "Hey, remember that handsome pilot, who flew us in the fog?" she writes. "Well, talk of the poetry of delays, we've gotten married. Yes we have, and I'm expecting our first in a few months' time!" The letter trembles in my hand until I read the au revoir. "Just a joke," it says.

SUITCASE

I'm on an old-fashioned train. I doze off to the gentle sway
of the wheels. I wake up. I blink. Then I sit bolt upright.
My suitcase is missing. I look around wildly. The train has
stopped, in the open countryside. I leap up and throw open
the sliding door and rush out into the passage, shouting for
the conductor. The carriage is deserted. So is the next one.
I come back and see the outside door of my compartment
open. I clamber down. A crowd of passengers is gathered by
the tracks a ways off. They watch the conductor kneeling
over an open suitcase, whose contents he is strewing over the
ground.

It's my suitcase. I give a shout and go running along the
side of the train. "That's mine!" I cry, as I come up breath-
lessly. "That's my suitcase! Someone stole it. What are you
doing — where did you find it?" The conductor looks up at
me mildly as I squat beside him. "This is yours, you say?"
he says. "Yes, yes," I assure him irritably, scrounging around
for my personal things and restoring them to semiprivacy
under the eyes of the crowd. "Someone made off with it
while I was asleep. Where did you find it?" "In your compartment," he says. "On the rack above you."

I turn my head and stare at him. "What are you saying?"
I demand. He shrugs. "You were asleep," he says. "We
didn't know whose it was." He gets to his feet. "Well whose

the hell did you think it was?" I protest, clapping the lid down and rising with the case clamped unlocked and dangling clothing under my arm. "You were asleep," he repeats, looking faintly amused. "We couldn't be sure." "Look, is this some kind of joke?" I snarl, flushing with anger. "So what if I was asleep?" "Now, now," says the conductor, holding up a hand, amiably. He glances over a shoulder and draws me away a few feet down the train from the other passengers.

"Tell me, have you ever been here before in this part of the country?" he asks confidentially. "What's that got to do with anything?" I retort. Over his shoulder I see the crowd inching forward to catch our words. I give them a glance. They look back at us, unabashed. "My point is," the conductor continues, angling his head with that amused, superior look that crinkles the sides of his eyes, "one more time, it makes people in these parts start wondering all sorts of things, when they see a young fellow like you, dozing away by himself like that."

I stare at him. I lift my head and stare at the faces beyond him. I come back to him, squaring my shoulders. My cheeks are aflame. " 'Things?' " I demand shrilly. "What 'all sorts of things?' My god, what allows you to make off with my personal property and go through it out here like a sideshow, because I dozed off? Something people have been doing in trains since they were invented!" The conductor shrugs. He grins at me. He doesn't speak. "I'm going to have you fired for this," I declare venomously. I shake a fist in his face. "I'm going to write a letter, and have you thrown out of the railroad! I've never been so insulted in my life!" I push him out of the way and stalk off balefully with my suitcase through the crowd, shouldering several aside as I go. I stop once to glare back at him.

The train moves off. I sit fuming in my compartment. I glower out at the countryside, which looks benign and hospitable as ever: tan and purple rolling hills, wide wandering streams, trim cottages set among stands of plump trees. I let out an oath and bang my fist on the seat beside me. "The insinuating bastard!" I hiss. "He's going to ruin my holiday!"

I shake myself. I get up and open the lid of the suitcase and start repacking it neatly. My blood boils, thinking of my private items strewn out like a yard sale by the side of the train, thinking of the expression on the conductor's face. "What the hell's the issue about my dozing off?" I protest out loud. No answer comes. The train hoots, and rushes along now into the hills.

UPRIVER

I buy passage on a mongrel steamer heading upriver. I negotiate the rickety planks to get aboard. The engine starts up, like a disgruntled pack animal forced back to labor. With a great how-do-you-do of churning, the steamer wallows out into the muddy stream, and commences our journey.

Belowdecks the dingy common room is close and reeks of fuel. My travelling companions are a couple of seedy business types, ubiquitous to this part of the world, I'll come to learn; an old stooped lawyer; and a prim, virginal young woman in a high-throated dowdy frock, no doubt going out to be a governess. I can't help eyeing her sidelong over our sticky table. She sits staring straight ahead in her torn chair, in an eerily rigid manner, without a word — without even, as far as I can tell, the slightest action of her frail breast. This behavior, and the pallor of her skin, make certain extravagant rumors I've heard play about in my mind.

"So is it true, what they say?" I begin, finding one of the businessmen out on the rusty deck, under a tattered wedge of canopy, where he fumigates the overripe twilight with the smoke of his cheroot. Adding it to the drifting sludgy wisps from the steamer's funnel. "I mean," I stammer on, "have you noticed the governess?"

He raises a bushy, scornful eyebrow at me. "How d'ya mean?" he says. I shift uncomfortably. I don't like him much at all. His florid jowls bulge over his too-tight collar, and the shoulders of his cheap jacket are popping at the seams. Even so I lean in close, smelling his sweat, and drop my voice. "I mean, I've heard," I begin again, "what with the climate out here — and the situation — I mean . . . is she . . . alive? I've heard — peculiar stories." I stare at him. "Do you think she might be stuffed?" I demand. "*Stuffed?*" he cries. He laughs, in distaste. "No, no, no," he says. "Drugged, maybe. Or more likely, put in a trance, poor wretch. To be awakened on arrival," he offers, "when they come to collect her." He snorts philosophically.

I blink. I turn slowly away from him, and stare off at the swarming bank of foliage across from us, now dimming in the tightening shroud of humid twilight. I swallow, laboriously, to try to rid my mouth again of the acrid taste of my fever pill. I blot at my brow with a rancid handkerchief, and smell the harsh drifts from the engine room, and the fumes of cigar. The river paws at our hull. "Yes, it's a brutal life out here, for a woman," my deckmate growls somewhere beside me. "Not half bad-looking either, I'd say. Once her blood's back moving." He grunts. "I wouldn't mind teaching her a thing or two," he informs me.

I keep silent in reply, tending the uneasy resonance of an image.

Around us the engine throbs, and groans, and drags us along deeper into the dark, choking walls of the wilderness, bearing in our midst the pale cargo of the governess, inert and transfixed in her cracked chair, like a feeble, desiccated figurehead, or a blighted icon, of our enterprise.

CARPET

I come into my hotel room with my small bag. I put it down by the bed and look around. The room is dowdy and old, with a nondescript view through the dingy lace of the curtains. The carpet is threadbare; it has an ominous concave area in the middle of it. Very carefully I crouch and lift back the carpet by an edge. I stiffen, involuntarily making a noise. I drop to my knees and peer down.

A hole gapes in the floorboards, giving on to a naked abyss, a chasm that dives away into an unfathomable yawning space in the earth. A dank breeze plays at my hair. With a thudding heart I stare at what I've disclosed. Then I reach over and spread the carpet again as it was, and sink back on my haunches, my fists clenched at my thighs as I collect myself. This carpet appears to be the false cover to a trap. One naive step, one careless turn — a person would plunge away into nothingness. I grunt to myself and shake my head with an intimate shiver. I run my hands through my disordered hair, and get to my feet and open the suitcase, to start putting some things in the chipped, flimsy bureau.

Then I go downstairs, to the hotel bar. I order dinner by myself at a small table by the wall. The place is shadowy, dull. There is only one other diner, a woman. I strike up a conversation with her. After dinner I buy her a drink at the dark little bar counter. She's pleasant enough, if much travelled, and likes to laugh. Her dress and coat are a bit worn.

"Why don't we go on up to my room," I suggest, a thought coming to mind as I look her over. "There's something I want to show you." The phrasing of the sentence provokes her to blink at me. A smile works her mouth. She bursts into a laugh.

We come into my room and I steer her blandly over to the side of the bed, to sit. I pour a couple of drinks from the bottle I have on the bureau. We salute. "So what is it you want to show me?" she says, with a tart hitch of her lip that's meant to be intimate and worldly. I look at her. In the lamplight, her features are coarsely etched. But there is an underlying vulnerability that stirs me, oddly, as it did downstairs. I sit beside her, and lean in and we kiss over our drinks. When we part, I take a deep breath. "Ready?" I ask. I can see the gravity of my tone confuses her. I climb down from the bed and edge along on my knees to the carpet. I'm a little drunk, and worked by a peculiar drift of emotion. She gazes down at me, baffled, trying to grin. I do the same. I throw back the carpet. She peers forward, then all at once she gasps.

Her drink splashes. She gives out a pathetic cry and scrambles wildly back along the bed against the wall, huddling away, crying out. Her reaction catches me unprepared. It shames me. I bring the carpet back and waddle over on my knees. I climb up beside her and put my arm around her, as she shudders and twists against the force of what she's seen. Her lipstick smears on my shirtsleeve. I smell her nondescript perfume and am gnawed by pathos.

She whimpers beside me, deeply wounded, like a terrified child. "Come now, you've seen worse," I murmur, stroking the brittle mass of her hair. "You've seen much worse in your time. . . ."

THE WELL

I climb into the big metal basket with my suitcase. I brace myself, swaying. I draw the lapels of my jacket around my throat and nod to the night attendant. He blinks at me torpidly and chews his lip. He begins to turn the handle of the winch. The winch is old and squeals painfully. I hunch my shoulders against the sound as I descend, slowly jarring, into the mouth of the well. The darkness of cobblestones closes over me, pierced by metal squeals. I mutter sarcastically at myself for this omen of my stay.

At length the basket jolts and stops. The bottom. I maneuver out, wrenching and twisting for space. I watch the clunky thatched vessel withdraw above me, like a slowly shrinking bird's nest being sucked away through a porthole of stars. I shout good night at the attendant, who cries something back, but the cobblestone echoes in manic incoherence. I grunt and shake myself. I fish out the heel of candle from my pocket. I strike a match and press the lighted candle into a perch on a stone. With grim unsurprise I look around me at the walls glistening in the flame light, and then up above. I shake my head, in rueful amusement. "So much for cheap vacations," I observe.

I crouch, and click open my suitcase. I change, shivering as I work myself out of my clothes into pajamas, nightgown, and slippers. Then I settle in, huddling on the flat suitcase against the cobblestones, with my jacket bundled up as a scratchy pillow.

The night deepens. I don't quite sleep, but grumble in semisleep. And these intimate sounds of mine wind upward in ricochet along the dank barrel of the well above me, and disperse into the open starry darkness. Other sounds do the same, from the other wells sunk all around in the landscape.

MAP

As dusk falls I come to a hamlet. It's just a few mean shacks really, grouped alongside the track. I pick out the least inhospitable-looking one, and arrange with the barefoot woman in the doorway for food and a place to spread my bedroll.

The evening turns into night, a massive operation in this part of the world, as if all nature was being laboriously shifted about, like an opera set. A plate of rice and beans is brought to me outside under the overhang of the brush-and-thatch roof. I eat, and put the plate aside, and bring out the map from its place in my rucksack. I spread it open in the weak flicker of the oil lamp. When the woman comes out for the plate, I ask her about the area marked on the map with the schoolboy iconography of an X. I describe the country to her, the way it was described to me. "I'm a sort of . . . prospector," I assure her, using the jaunty term from the local lingo, to set her at ease about my presence here. I mention nothing about a long-lost personal relic. She glances frowning at the map a moment, and dully shakes her head. Obviously map and description mean nothing to her. She shakes her head a further time, and goes back inside.

For a while longer I sit with the open map on my knee. I estimate as best I can another three or four days before I make any kind of arrival. If nothing intervenes, that is, which is a hollow piece of faith in this part of the country. Slowly I fold up the map and its painstaking whorls and dotted approximations, and stow them all carefully back in the rucksack.

Then I sit forward with my elbows on my knees. There is the telltale noise of a waterfall somewhere nearby, a steady unwavering roar above the pulse and chuckle of the unlit night. The woman comes back out with a bottle and a glass for me, and a glass of her own. She sits on the other overturned metal drum. It's her place, after all. She pours for herself, and sips without ceremony. I sit with my empty glass in hand, after a perfunctory nod to manners of lifting it in the air. The night quakes around us. I ask the woman idly about the waterfall. She shrugs blankly. "Is it big?" I persist, because of her way. She shrugs again, as if to say maybe bigger than one, smaller than another. Or that she couldn't be bothered to know. I look at her. She drinks. I pour a little from the bottle and consider the turbid liquid in my glass. And she really knows nothing, I press again, nothing about the place of which I inquired? I try to describe it once more, fretfully, taking pains to be as simple and vivid in my terms as possible. She shakes her head all the while I'm talking. When I'm done she stares ahead into the darkness.

Finally she turns slowly toward me. Her eyes are dark brown and cloudy. "The waterfall about which you ask," she says. Where would I say it is, she wants to know. "Why, somewhere over there," I tell her, pointing. She nods at this, with the show of a strange, unamused smile. "Yes," she says. "Tonight. That is where it is. But last night . . ." She raises a worn hand, and indicates an entirely different direction.

MONSTERS

I hire a girl and a car and driver, and we head off from the hotel area for the evening's viewing. I give directions, per the concierge. The car is old, badly sprung, the road barely more than a track scratching its way in our weak headlights along the ominous coast. Below, the ocean seethes and lurches in. The moon is up, a stained lamp throwing queasy light across the landscape. We pass some shabby huts, long abandoned by the locals, where a few of the more reckless tourists have set up station. Gaunt figures watch from hammocks as we grind past through a curve. They wave to us, in a stupor. Our running boards scrape on the ruts. I sit against the old pocked window, staring out. The girl runs her hand along my leg, and then works the bottle from my grasp, to help herself. The liquor is genuine, and cost me good money.

"Are we anywhere near there?" I call out irritably to the driver.

"Soon, soon," he assures me. He speeds up to show his acuteness to my wishes. Then he cries out, jabbing with a whole arm at the night off to my side. I press my face hard to the window.

A swath of trees has been battered and torn apart, mercilessly bludgeoned into stumps and splinters. Appallingly, as if from the rampage of a giant primeval tail. I swallow in agitation. I glance at the girl. Roughly, I take the bottle back from her. She yelps in protest, and slaps at me. I cuff her back. She cries out, and slumps away against the door at her side. The driver watches in concern in his mirror. "Go on, but slower," I instruct him. "And don't scare them off!" I warn. I lean forward, peering, bottle swaying in hand. The car feels its way along, jostling at a crawl. Its running boards grind. All at once it jolts violently to a halt.

I go lurching into the seat back. I curse. The driver hisses over his shoulder and motions at the windshield. I strain to see ahead into the faint spill of the lights. The engine under the hood rumbles and wheezes, like a broken-down animal, panting in distress here at the edge of a wide gully. All at once a dull roar thunders in the engulfing darkness. The car seems to tremble. "There —" blurts the driver. I clench my fists. My heart throbs. Two monstrous silhouettes lurch into view above the rim of the far side of the gully. They're heads, the size of beach shacks. They rise, bobbing from side to side, on the tops of emerging shoulder masses, scaly and hairy. The stupendous heads pause, glitter-eyed. We gasp in the car as a gargantuan tail erupts, and retreats. Something leaps into the moonlight from a head, like a dancing snake, then glides back into its home jaws. High tiny eyes flash. I press openmouthed, taut, against the car door. The girl's hand clutches my thigh.

The monsters drift away, shoulders disappearing under the horizon, then heads. Then, silence.

The car engine howls, we veer backward in a furious arc, swing about, and pitch and sway off in the shafts of headlights again.

"What's wrong?" I demand. "Where are we going?"

"What?" says the driver. "You see some, now we go back."

"No, no," I protest. "I paid for more!" We haggle. Our argument turns nasty. The driver insists he has provided service and entertainment as negotiated, I inform him I am entitled to more. He stops the car. The liquor heats my temper. I threaten him. He seethes. The girl breaks in that she knows another location nearby. "Much better," she declares. "So where is it?" I demand. She gives the name. The driver shakes his head, vehemently. "No, no," he says. "Too dangerous." "Nonsense," I tell him. "I want to go there. Drive." The driver lifts his hands conspicuously away from the wheel in reply. More threats from me, including the specter of a formal complaint, which will cost him his license. Finally with this last threat, and the girl's negotiation that he receive an additional fee, he puts the car in gear. As I repocket my billfold, the suspicion all at once crosses my mind that the two of them might be in league together. I brood over this.

The girl has the bottle again. I take it back and I drink, while she presses against me and whispers some canned phrases about the thrilling sights awaiting us. I handle her through her thin, tawdry dress and smell the crude scent of her flesh in the stale inert odor of the car.

We bump along on the route by which we'd come, and then reach a rough, meager crossroads. The driver halts. We don't move. The girl snaps at him. I add a barked command. Reluctantly the gears engage; we rumble onto a narrow neck of rocky track, toward a promontory that juts into the waves. It's obvious now why the driver thinks the site too dangerous. We'll be surrounded on three sides by the ocean's roar, where the great beasts can erupt spraying and screeching over us at close quarters. With only this fragile, rutted link to the safety of shore. One, two, sweeps of a monstrous tail against the pontoon of rocks behind us, and we're trapped.

The car heaves along with only its dim low beams now. The driver squirms in his seat and opens and closes his fingers on the wheel nonstop. Finally we slow, and stop. We cut our lights. The dark rubble of the shore drops away ahead and on both sides. The waves stagger heavily in, thundering, and churn in agitation, in struggle. The driver mutters prayers under his breath. My heart hammers in me, so I can barely breathe. This is what I came to this wayward coast for. I swallow from the bottle as the girl clutches on to me. I can feel her chest pulse against my shoulder, and I grip her bare knee roughly. We stare out the windows, at the dark agitated waves. In the spellbound car, the driver's murmuring drones in the waiting silence.

Visit

VISIT

I undertake a perilous journey, and go visit my brother. I feel the thorn of fraternal guilt. It's been over two years, I've lost touch completely. My brother is a family man and proud of it. On quivering legs I knock on the door of his big ungainly house on a suburban street. With half-averted eyes I return his embrace and greet again his wife, and his two young children, who are his true glory. "See how they've grown since last time," he declares, with a grin that unabashedly levels hurt and admonition and pride at me. I mutter something and return his embrace again, which is misty-eyed with sentiment.

Before dinner we sit in his backyard by the swing set and the rhododendron bush. Over dietetic beer in the twilight, he charts the improvements to his property, house and acreage. A painter's ladder leans against the rear siding. He regards me. He smiles a certain way. "What's so funny?" I ask. "Nothing," he says. "Do you always dress, you know, that way?" "You've never seen plus fours?" I answer. "Walking shoes? They're what a traveller wears. What's so *funny?*" I demand. He's laughing. He starts to say something, but breaks off. "Never mind," he says. "Sorry. Here." He comes back from a wan overgrown little area by the driveway gate. I taste his homegrown tomato, which is wan and bland. "Good," I tell him, playing the guest. "There's nothing like eating vegetables you've grown yourself," he

says. He looks at me again. "What?" I demand. He shakes
his head. He tries to suppress a smile. I feel myself sim-
mering. I look off at the dim grass, tight jawed.

Over dinner his wife asks me the same intrusive questions she always does. I shrug and mumble. My brother
watches our dialogue with protective domestic intentness,
and vulnerability. I get loose of his wife's probing by fetch-
ing my battered suitcase, to give the children their presents:
two brass coins featuring Asiatic profiles; two toy creatures
starkly carved from wood. The animals seem slight and
shabby here in the dining room light, when they were so
bright and festive at the market stall where I bought them.
The children blankly pronounce thank-you's. I try to stoke
the glamour of my gifts by spinning yarns of the faraway
places I bought them, the times I had en route. The wanderer's bent for relics, the magic of mementos. My brother's
wife laughs nervously. "They have a peculiar aroma," she
says. My brother looks on with a grin, biding his time for his
own presentation. He turns away, biting his lip, as the little
boy demands why I dress like I do — and why I always
seem to travel alone. I fabricate some kind of reply, coloring.

In the living room my brother spreads out his newest
trove of snapshots on the coffee table, and with his little girl
on his knee, he leads a practiced tour of his own latest travels, which are always to fine places, surrounded by col-
leagues, new friends and their kids, freshly unearthed
distant relatives. With a conspicuous patience he answers
his children's questions in pedagogic singsong. I look off
sidelong at the carpet and count the minutes until bedtime
on the faux-copper mantel clock. To close the evening he
brings out old photos he has found of the two of us. I gaze at
the familiar iconography: my brother forthrightly addressing the camera, almost hungrily sentimental and bon-

homous, his arm around me to proclaim the occasion. Myself glancing away and down, moody and ill at ease, palpa-
bly unhappy. "Uncle, why do you always look so miserable?"
the little boy asks. I force a genial, put-upon laugh. I yawn.

I'm shown my room, in the back on the second floor. It's
small and airless and smells of new paint. Laundry and
books and papers wedge against a wall. "It is lovely," I agree,
at my brother's proud explanation of its future as his new
study. I suffer our good-night and the promise of a real
heart-to-heart tomorrow, and I close the ill-fitting door and
sink onto the pilled bedclothes with my head in my hands.
My suitcase balances its patchwork of labels and ragged
straps on top of the laundry basket. Like a hapless artifact
of a shabby, scorned religion. I reach for the lamp switch
and lie back slowly in the darkness. I feel numb.

I try to sleep, but the air is too close. In the middle of
the night I can't take it anymore. Any of it. I rise and
furtively get into my slighted plus fours. I push my suitcase
ahead of me through the little window, and I squirm out
after it onto the lower roof. A big moon rides in the darkness over the silhouette of my brother's chimney. I scan the
dark backyards on either hand. Warily I inch along down
the new shingles to the painter's ladder, and climb fearfully
onto it with my suitcase, and make my way down the rungs.

I creep over to the black skeleton of the swing set. I sit
and prepare to bed there on the just-cool badly mown grass,
until dawn, when I'll make my getaway. Crickets scrape all
around. I gaze up at the dark stories of my brother's sleeping house, the citadel of his ways and his pride. I decide to
crawl under the rhododendron, so as not to be spied from
any of the windows. For good measure I go around behind
the bush, between it and the back fence. Then I stop. I peer
squinting on all fours.

A dim stone step leads down into the earth under the dark rear brow of the rhododendron. I lean back out and direct an amazed glance up at the sleeping house.

I follow the dark rocky narrow steps, in disbelief, slowly down, down, through narrow walls. I emerge into the front chamber of a cavern. It's a bit lighter here. I make my way forward with my suitcase, pressing along the wall to keep my footing on loose rock. All at once the cavern yawns wide, into a vast subterranean expanse. Half-light wobbles on the surface of water. "My god," I blurt in awe. Before me a lake stretches away into the obscure distance. I hurry down on the crunching sand of a little beach. I stand peering out, and then scan for a path along the limestone shore, whose pale contours show in the dim light.

"Uncle!" cry a pair of voices.

I whirl about. My brother's kids look at me from a dozen yards away. They're on a smooth stretch of rock, in their pajamas. "What are you doing here?" asks the girl, as I approach. "What are you two doing here?" I retort in turn, astonished, and alarmed, both for their safety and at their encountering me just when I'm about to slip out of their lives again. "You're the only real-live grown-up who's ever found this place," announces the boy. "Well, I guess that's because I'm not quite like other grown-ups," I hear myself reply simply. The cliché sounds proud and magical in my ears, but also feeble in a way, sad and pathetically defiant. "Your mom and dad don't know you're here?" I demand, using concern to reassert myself. "Of course not," says the boy. "It's dad's mom and dad who showed it to us."

I stare at him. My legs quiver.

"My parents are here? Now?" I gasp. I turn right and left. "Of course not," says the girl. "They're ghosts. They only came just once, last summer. To see what their grandchildren were like." I stare down at them. "They were scary," says the boy. "We could see right through them. But they were very nice, they showed us this secret place under our yard." "We came down here 'cause we couldn't sleep," says the girl. "We wanted to play with our gifts." And before me they hold up in display, gripped tightly, my coins in one hand, my crudely whittled creatures in the other. For some reason, emotion stabs through me. I drop to a knee and pull them to me in my arms and kiss them on their heads. A tear prickles down my cheek. "You cry, just like dad does," says the boy. "Do I?" I murmur, brushing the tear away. "When you come back from where you're going now," he goes on, "will you bring us more presents?" I sit back on my heel, and I smile at him, touched and shamed by his request, and by his perspicacity about my suitcase being with me. "Bigger and better ones," I promise. "Uncle, is this a pony or a dog?" asks the girl with concern, waggling the item in question. I grin at her softly. "Which do you prefer?" I ask. "Uncle," the boy interrupts, "before you go now where you're going, can you take us for a ride in the rowboat?"

I swing around toward where he points. I clamber to my feet in surprise. A skiff bobs at the foot of the beach. Shipped oars stick up from a gunwale. Somehow I missed all of this before. "Jesus," I mutter, taking a step to confirm my senses. Then I whirl back.

I announce my leave, promising I'll take them for a grand ride my next visit. "But right now Uncle has to be going," I explain, stooping over them, hand on my suitcase. "To get an early start on his journey. And you two have to get back to your house," I tell them. "We don't want your mom and dad finding your beds empty." " 'Cause they'll be worried," says the girl. With a touch of petulance, her brother begs still for a short spin. I raise my eyebrows at him, and a finger, and tell him tenderly but firmly, I'm sorry: next time. He grumbles in protest. "Come on," says the girl, taking him by the arm. I give them a kiss good-bye. I admonish them to go carefully up the dark steps. The girl reaches into her pajama waist and produces a bright yellow little flashlight, which she displays in answer. I laugh in admiration.

I watch the two of them start back, the girl leading dutifully, the boy slouching in disappointment. At the chamber entry they both turn and wave vigorously, clutching their presents. "Good-bye, Uncle!" they cry, in their pajamas. I shout back a valediction, and blow a kiss, and waving I turn and tramp down to the skiff. I climb in and set the oars. I look down at my suitcase, pocked but stalwart and durable between my darned corduroy knees and the worn heels of my brogues. I take a deep breath and my heart surges through me. I start to maneuver around. Then I stop.

I jump swaying to my feet. I shout back at the children, who are still there, watching from the entrance. I flap my hands at them to be off. Their tiny voices call out again to me. Finally they turn and do as told. The dim light of their flashlight flickers a moment.

I wait to make sure they're gone. Then I sit again and grab the oars. I wheel the boat around. I gaze out over my shoulder at the scene of my journey lying ahead. I blow out another starting breath, and I begin pulling. Slowly I watch the little beach, and the cavern entrance beyond, under my brother's backyard, grow smaller and smaller at each stroke. The burdens of my visit shrink away with them. I keep the nose of the boat parallel to the limestone shore. I round the first headland. I pause for just another moment to survey the distances ahead, feeling once again *at home,* on my way to strange places.

BUBBLE

I take a ride on a bubble. I mount up on a leaf in the giant's garden. It's a young man's game, but I join the weekend daredevils who sneak in here while the giant snores in his tower of boulders. The wide breeze blows across the morning dew and the bubbles swell into being, and I wait my turn to clamber onto one, like a jockey, squeezing an iridescent perch between my knees. Then the breeze freshens, and I give a yelp of alarm and joy, and wobble aloft into the sunlight.

Around me the whooping, jostling flock of bubbles navigate the current. Most of us sport a honeysuckle trumpet-blossom as an airstreamed cap, and motorist's goggles and trailing white scarf, and the herringbone plus fours which are the bubble riders' borrowing from our earthbound cousins, the bicyclists. We stream down pell-mell over the lawn and terraces, over the nodding treasuries of roses and the high stands of pink gladiolas in the flower beds.

A few calculating souls always try to outsmart the haphazardness of our flight — rigging themselves with strutted wings on their backs, or with thin airfoils strapped and cinched to their ankles. One of them comes suddenly scuttling up through the midst of us. Shouts and curses pursue him as others clamor out of his way. I watch another ambitious sort go slowly whirling down into the lily pads of the stone pool. The rotor blade of his elaborate headpiece bounces away on the flagstones. Over it comes drifting a newcomer who's somehow got himself astoundingly inside his bubble. He gapes out through the glossy membrane in a state of panic and idiotic laughter. A gust of breeze sends him flailing, like a fetus resisting birth, toward the epic tangled bulk of a greengage plum tree.

I lean into this same gust of air, steering with my knees and tugging hands. I rise, banking unsteadily, and make a wavering course for the towering eaves of the giant's house. Some fearless types are there already, hovering outside the giant's window for a glimpse of the monster abed. For the first time I myself bob beside them, and through their milling honeysuckle caps I claim my debut sight of the behemoth in his den. Yellow-check curtains form a proscenium on the scale of an opera set. I blink through in trepidation and awe at something like a haystack, which makes a rumbling like an iron cartwheel over cobblestones. It's the giant's snoring head, with its fearsome one eye closed in the center of its brow, and its blond nettle patch of beard.

"He seems so young!" I reflect, tracing the huge bare arm tha , trails to the floor over a homespun blanket resembling a small plot of field. Beneath immense fingers lies the remains of an ox carcass, easily much bigger than — "than a man," I uneasily calculate.

A new gust rocks me, and starts to spin me about. "Careful, idiot —" voices erupt around me, as one of the more foolhardy riders is almost swept in over the sill. His mates grapple with him, and shove him off wobbling into the safety of blazing ivy beside the window ledge.

I turn from them, exulting. I bank around in the

direction of the garden once more. My heart is in triumph.
I've stolen an unauthorized, intimate view of the giant, and
am alive to tell it! I feel newly bold, vital — capable even
of tackling the far lower wall. To ride my glistening bubble
out beyond the garden! This is the real escapade, it forgoes
the soft landings of turf and leafy bushes for the pavements
and slate roofs, and other hazards, of the village. And the
village folk don't take happily to young men in honey-
suckles tumbling out of the sky onto their church bazaars
and shop awnings and laundry lines. Putting at risk, what's
more, their peaceable relations with the giant on his hill.

I've always felt daunted by the challenge of sailing the
village. But now, I'm ready for my maiden jaunt.

The broad overgrown lip of the wall looms there before
me. A giant tuft of dandelion floats up close. I maneuver out
of its path, and hurriedly wiggle a surer perch, and shout at
the small knot of bubble riders ahead to clear the way. One
of them looks back around at me, contemptuous of the
alarm in my voice. I crane forward, jockey style, and my
heart lunges in me — and a cross breeze bumps me veering
slowly at a downward angle, toward the brambles on the
wall top. I writhe frenziedly, straining to buck the sinking
bubble aloft. "Don't struggle, man, don't struggle!" calls a
young guy hovering expertly a few yards off. He has a half
halo of daisy petals sportively fringing his honeysuckle. I
bleat in horror, as I drift right down onto the brambles. My
bubble squashes under my weight. A thorny twig juts up
into the membrane beneath me, and the whole glistening
carapace sinks in slow motion toward it. "Don't struggle!"
the voice repeats . . . but I couldn't if I wanted — I'm par-
alyzed, awaiting the explosive pop to send me floundering
into the depths of the thorns.

And then, in reciprocal slow motion, the bubble's tensile strength holds, and pauses, and then begins to swell — and I bounce spellbound from the brambles back up into the air, and out over the garden wall. "Way to go, gramps!" cries the advising voice. I glance over my shoulder with an ashen grin, and flip a quick, vulgar gesture of triumph back, with a trembling hand.

I ride bobbing on down toward the rooftops of the village. I gulp in exhilaration and fumble at my honeysuckle cap and goggles, awry from my struggles. I readjust the clasp of my knees. Below unwinds the little river, along whose banks I've gone poking along many a weekend morning like this one. Some fishermen are there with their sons. The boys point up at me in excitement, the men scowl and spit and call their sons back to their lines in the water. I laugh. In high spirits I lean sideways, and bank a course for the village center. The rushing wind makes ocean noises in my ears, my honeysuckle cap quivers. A pair of sharp-beaked robins swoop dangerously alongside. I wave them off with a flurry of my hand.

Now the steeple of the church rises. A rummage sale crowds the lawn behind it. I can't restrain myself, I execute a bumpy show-off circle around the steeple's upright, like a windborne none-too-safe carousel ride. Shouts of scandal erupt below. Shakily I whiz glistening back and forth over sellers and buyers and tables, then make off yelping for the library. En route the open mouths of chimneys, and other fearsome places to lose altitude, stare up at me. I stare back. I pass over my own address before I know it, and I manage a brief steep glimpse through my very window, and I shout for joy.

I turn recklessly, careening onto the main street, and

swoop low over honking cars and wave back at a pair of girls who've run out of the pastry shop to salute me and my bubble. Distracted, I look up just in time to avoid a bristling TV antenna. I veer off, heeling over, onto a tree-lined street of small houses. I battle a gust, and a kid comes scrambling along below me with predatory persistence on his upturned face. "Hey! —" I shout, as he aims on the run with his sling-shot. He fires. "You crazy little —" I snarl, jerking franti-cally to change course. I skid off over a driveway, but there's a second shot.

Like a crystalline hiccup, the bubble pops.

I come heavily to earth on top of a garage overhang. I gasp. A screen door bangs open just below. An old fellow storms out. "You heedless flower-headed fools!" he rasps, shaking a scrawny fist. "Look at my rainspout — I'll teach you something! Why, you're a grown man," he squawks. "You should be ashamed of yourself!" He disappears inside. I struggle hurriedly, grunting, to clamber off. As I start to hang by my hands, something stings me in the back of my neck so I yell and loose my grip, and tumble violently to the ground.

I hobble off under the shade trees, in my dented honey-suckle and dirty plus fours, cursing after the kid who keeps up his gleeful, taunting fusillade on the run. The old guy fills in the rear of this tableau of the three ages of man. He brandishes an ax, wheezing along in fury after me.

And on this sour, chaotic note, my aerial joyride comes to its end.

SILK

The day dawns cloudy, drizzly. I hire a sampan. We start off for the lesser of the two islands in the famous lake out beyond the waterways of the city. I wear a trench coat, with the collar turned up, and a fedora. The outfit suits my mission, I reflect, indulging in one more piece of romantic fancy, to go along with the rest. The sampan man works his oar in his dingy cloak. I think again of the girl, last night in the rattan shadows of the bar . . . her opal eyes, lacquered floral smile . . . the silk of her bare throat above the scarlet sheath of her silk dress . . . the blaze of a chrysanthemum in the jet gloss of her hair. A full week of such allure has brought me to this — a surreptitious mission of vague but apparently urgent local import. Of course I said yes, after the briefest twinge of alarm. I have a tourist's naive arrogance, his heedless taste for intrigue and adventure. I'm a would-be lover who scents a display of bravado will clinch the deal.

We draw up under droopy willows, to a small stone landing. I make sign language for the sampan man to wait in the shadows. Beyond, at the top of worn-away stone stairs, rises the fog-shrouded old pagoda. I mount carefully. The stone is vertiginously slick with moss and damp. I pass florid growths of dripping chrysanthemums. I reach the pagoda terrace, breathing somewhat noisily. The old shrine is silent,

famously deserted for years. Mold has invaded its lacquered
shingles, rotted away chunks of the scalloped beam work
and eaves rafters overhead. I walk to the corner on the right,
and turn. More empty terrace, fog. I take a breath and cough
twice, emphatically, which is the signal. There's silence. I
look around uncertainly behind me, lifting a quizzical eyebrow. When I turn back, I give a start.

A figure looks up at me: short and slight, shorn headed.
He wears the lavender cloak of a monk. He regards me
gravely through thick, primitive spectacles. He opens his
mouth. He coughs, once. I respond softly but emphatically:
"God bless you." There's a pause. He reaches into his cloak,
spectacles fixed on me all the while. Suddenly it strikes me
what a labor it must be for him to keep his glasses clear in
this sort of weather, and I have to fight the urge to giggle.
I take the paper packet from him, its closed flap graceful
with colored traceries. God knows what's inside. I push the
object of my mission into the inside pocket of my trench
coat. The monk blinks at me. He turns. He slips away into
the fog around the corner.

I stand for a moment, gazing amused after him. Then I
remember I'm to leave at once. Heart thumping a bit, I
creep back along the terrace, making a little joke of it, rising on tiptoe. I start down the first precipitous steps.

An odd scream erupts somewhere behind me.

I freeze. I twist about. There's no more sound, no more
explanation but fog and silence. I look back past the collar
of my trench coat down the stairs. The sampan is out of
sight still, under the willows. Heart pounding, I take another step down toward it. I stop. I look around behind me.
On a reckless impulse, I creep back up to the terrace.
"Hello?" I call hesitantly. I edge along hearing the damp

dripping from the beams, the pulse in my ears. I reach the corner, and peer around. Only fog. I take a step and then a voice jolts me from behind.

I turn, arms in the air. The sampan man stares up at me. He has a small black gun in his grip. He thrusts his free hand toward me, palm up. There is glossy blood on the sleeve above it. I swallow. I purse my lips, but I have no choice. I reach into my trench coat and haughtily bring out the ornamented packet. He snatches it from me and glances at it, hard eyed. He steps back. He waves the gun to signal me inside.

The interior of the pagoda still smells of sandalwood, but only faintly. The tang of mildew and mold fills my nostrils. After ten minutes I sit on the floor, against the scroll-work of a ceremonial teak cabinet. My hands are tied behind me, partly by myself in fact, at the dumb-show coaching of the sampan man. The thought ludicrously occurs to me that my trench coat, fresh from the usury of the hotel dry cleaners, will have to go right back there again thanks to the state of the planked floor. Amused, I feel my tourist's sangfroid getting back into the swing of things. I snort to myself, wryly deriding where intertwining enthusiasms have led me.

There's a coded tap on the door. The sampan man stiffens. He raises his gun, and after an exchange of whispers with the outside, he opens up. The girl steps in. She is clad in a day version of her silk sheath, with a scarf stamped with chrysanthemums in place of the blossom itself. She glances over. She walks slowly across the hollow-ringing planks, and stands gazing down at me. She smiles, floral mouthed. "You don't seem very surprised," she says.

I smile back under the brim of my fedora. A pang of

desire and admiration glamorizes the whole scene, inspires me. "Well, I've had time to think a few things over," I reply suavely. "Sitting here nice and easy like this." The girl lifts back her scarfed head and laughs. She nods, in salute to my coolness. "You've been most gallant . . . and useful," she says. She considers me. She looks over her slender shoulder and snaps a remark at the sampan man. He answers. She seems satisfied. I cross my outstretched legs. "I just don't quite understand. . . ." I drawl, an amateur with a feel for the big game. "Why the need for me? Why a go-between for that package from that poor monk? Who's dead now, I take it?" "We didn't need you," the girl replies evenly, ignoring my last question. Scorn plays lightly in her opal eyes. "We needed your room," she says.

I blink. She laughs. "To plant a little bomb," she says. "Oh, just big enough to blow out a few windows, just enough of a disturbance for the fools in charge of the city to rush over, thinking the target of our sabotage is there." I swallow. "Whereas the real bomb goes off somewhere else," I murmur, reverberating. She nods, with a sardonic hitch of red lips. "You see, all that fanciful reading you like to go on about in bars hasn't been for naught," she declares. "No doubt," I mutter, a trace of bitterness intruding on my manner, "you've planted 'just enough' evidence to implicate me, as a provocateur. Which means the guillotine, according to the newspapers." She smiles, and dips her scarfed head and its array of blossoms.

She glances back at the sampan man. "Now we really must be going," she says. "Of course we have to make sure you don't run off and raise an alarm. . . ." "Of course," I echo. I grin, wanly. I take a breath, which turns deeper and more tremulous than I intended. She brings a small red paper purse from behind her waist. The sight of it unnerves me. "Is this — necessary?" I hear myself blurt, as a needle glints in her hand, with a spool of silk. She titters, sounding just a moment like the cocktail dream in the bar last night. She leans in, fragrantly, so I draw away. "Now, now," she says. "Too bad you've never had your ears pierced. Please don't struggle, you'll just make things more painful and difficult." The sampan man has come up and stands behind her, stonily watching. I gnash a curse as the needle goes in. My heels gouge at the floor planks.

Fifteen minutes pass. My fedora lies upended by my leg. Fine lines of silk run from my earlobes to hooks in either side of the cabinet behind me. Drops of blood ruin the shoulders of my trench coat. I grit my teeth against the stinging pain, the humiliation of being trussed like a dog in cobwebs. I force a stiff-necked, feeble but defiant wink, as the girl appraises her silken handiwork, back upright. "Delicate, but insidiously *effective*," she announces, her head angled in the pose of a connoisseur. "Like so much of our culture, don't you think? Now truly we must go," she says. "But how can I leave, without a parting gift . . . to the promise of our intimacy?" She lifts her plucked brows, mocking. She extends a lacquer-tipped finger. She traces it along my cheek. I growl. She stoops.

The fingertip wanders down my trench coat, until it reaches my trousers. My eyes widen. I feel my fly being unbuttoned. I gasp. The girl kneels in her glossy sheath, and starts to lower her floral mouth, smiling opal eyes pinned on me. I gulp back at her. The sampan man clatters up. He cries out, scandalized. His sweeping arm indicates our context. The girl flaps him away. She snarls at him over her shoulder. I see him retreat, and then step outside, noisily flinging the door shut. The girl turns back to me. Her opal eyes are narrowed, smirking, flagrant. "Jesus — what are you —" I sputter. The silk stings my ears as I contort and squirm, all vestige of the debonair fled. My heels scrape at the floor planks.

It's the wounds I can show in my earlobes, sullenly, that save my tourist neck some time afterward.

AT SEA

I book passage on a tramp freighter. I'm the only person-age of this type aboard. My amenities are rudimentary: a closet-sized cabin I have to myself. Through my leaky porthole I watch the rocky coast dwindle between the grindstones of sea and sky.

I take my meals with captain and crew, a dour and hardened lot. There is little chitchat at our rolling, high-seas table, little food for what I'm after. No salty yarns of exotic ports, no recollections of strange disasters followed by a celebratory chantey. Just the clank of cheap mismatched spoons, the slurp of bean soup echoed by the slosh of waves against the hull. The glug of resinous wine being drained from tumblers in hairy fists that aren't all that clean. Even an aggressive, careless belch or two.

There is so little colorfully nautical atmosphere, in fact, that after a few days of it, I realize I've made a terrible mistake: my absurdly misguided notion of the romance of life aboard ship has stuck me with this white elephant of a journey. I turn over a request for an emergency interview with the captain.

He beats me to it. I find myself in his quarters, in the glare of a kerosene lamp, with old charts rolled up on the floor or taped in slovenly fashion to the bulkheads. "I know you must find us not very amiable and festive company," he

declares point-blank, sucking at his greasy pipe. "Hardly
the glorious pageant of working sea life you no doubt an-
ticipated!" I'm thrown off by his candor. "No, no," I hear
myself protest, coloring. "I've actually, really, sort of en-
joyed —" "Because," he goes on, removing his pipe and
leaning forward suddenly, "because we are proceeding
under conditions you do not comprehend. How could you?"
he demands, rhetorically. "But now it is necessary, by the
courtesies of the sea, that we offer a glimpse of an explanation — to you, our passenger!"

He calls out a name toward the door. The second mate
appears, a gruff type in a low, dirty stocking cap, with
coarsely unshaven cheeks. The captain barks something in
their native tongue. The second mate starts. He growls and
looks at me and shakes his head. The captain barks again.
The second mate scowls harder. He looks more adamant.
"Listen, please, it's really not nece —" I start to announce,
much discomforted. The captain rises and claps his hands
sharply. The second mate angrily reaches up and grabs hold
of both his ears under his cap, and jerks. I squawk. His face
distorts hideously, and then comes away in his hands. My
shout stops in my throat. A wealth of jet-black hair gleams
free in the stark lamplight.

A magnificent girl glares at me, her almond eyes proud
and defiant at her extraordinary unveiling.

"Now you understand," declares the captain, as I sit
there openmouthed and wide-eyed. "We are not exactly
what we seem. I trust you know something of the hostilities in our poor suffering part of the world," he goes on. "We
are a special contingent of female partisans, transporting il-
legal but vitally needed arms to a safe port. Where they will
find their way," he exclaims, "to our heroic comrades!" I

blink. I nod, spellbound by the dark-haired transmutation before me. My whole notion of this voyage has graphically altered.

The captain roughly dismisses the ersatz mate. She slouches out the peeling metal door, muttering something fierce as she does and shooting a glance at me.

The door shuts. The captain picks up his pipe and eyes me. "My friend," he announces. "You are the only man on a ship of beautiful and courageous women in disguise, in the middle of the ocean! Myself included." He leans forward again. "Just don't get any fancy ideas," he says. I nod, again. "Of course not," I assure him. "I mean — 'of course.' Not. What I mean —"

Back in my cabin, I lie on my itchy bunk blanket in a state of sleepless mania, my head throbbing with consensual jet-haired free-for-all's, with mass unmaskings and salt-air familiarities, all to the sluggish thump of the waves.

I spend the next strange intense morning roving the decks and gangways with new eyes. Knots of seamen look back over their dirty cable-knit shoulders at me, and nod sullenly, and go about their business of swabbing and hauling. Coiling yards of tarry rope. I turn away from them with a distracted grin out at the briny miles, hearing the roar in my ears, from my pulse. I debate the expense of treating everyone to extra wine rations at lunch. I lean over the rail and strain for a stolen peep of the second mate among the stanchions.

A short hour later the captain puts a shocking end to my idyll. I'm back in his quarters. A grimy radio crackles in the corner. There've been developments overnight, I am informed. More contraband must be taken on immediately, my shoebox of cabin space will be needed. I'm to be put ashore, with a refund. I protest frantically. "I'll be happy to share quarters with the crew," I announce, and realize immediately the implications. "I mean I'll sleep on deck!" I desperately amend myself. "I don't care — please! I don't care!"

But the captain won't hear of it. By suppertime I go lurching with my bags down the gangway onto a crude shadowy wharf. A load of big heavy boxes come trundling back up to take my place. The freighter casts off. I run alongside as it slips out of my life, like a beautiful dream glimpsed only at its beginning, then broken off by the harsh gloom of day. I wave my arms, throwing pent-up kisses at the stolid pea-jacketed figures at the rail. "I'll wait for you," I shriek, over and over. The second mate gives a limp, indeterminate flap back, as the ship's details recede into just a bulk, then a lanterned blob, then part of the darkness.

I stay on in this forlorn mooring for a month, scrabbling through the badly printed newspaper once a week for intelligence about the hostilities. I haunt the wharfmaster's one-room shack for bulletins of comings and goings. On a desperate inspiration, I book passage on another freighter, and after an embarrassment there, another. Still more embarrassment.

Finally I realize my dream is lost. And for longer than I care to say, I become one of those landmen who haunt the fringes of the waves . . . whose hearts have been lost to the sea. Hours on end they scan the empty tides, waiting, praying, for the sight of one certain smoke funnel on the horizon. I sigh, and tramp back and forth among them, under the screams of the gulls.

SNOW: A TALE OF THE OLD NORTH

A storm strands me in the old northern capital. For days and nights on end the snow flies thick and fast, and the wind howls, swirling the big flakes in dancing, blinding veils, piling up monumental drifts. Only the cries of a few indomitable sleigh men rise from the narrow tormented streets to the window of my chamber. The wind makes tatters of their foolhardy curses, the cracks of their whips, the complaints of their struggling ponies.

Then the weather clears, and the old capital is left clogged and muffled with white. Snow drapes the gilded onion domes and tiled spires like a form of ponderous arctic moss. The local populace comes out, laboring through the drifts between the slovenly wooden houses and the grand stone buildings. These splendid edifices boast imported fancies of ornamentation, of sun-drenched pastel plasterwork magnificent with scrolls and other such prodigies of adornment. Everywhere is fur — voluminous fur hats, thick fur coats and collars, fur boots. The sleighs rock and bump through the scene, rudely making way. The sleigh men lay about defiantly with their whips and oaths. A stunning cold settles in. The smoke from chimneys piles up solid and immobile in the frozen air.

My hosts are minor nobility. Their great house is drafty, dating from the capital's earliest age of prosperity. But it's comfortable for all that, richly hung with carpets and tapestries, and the ware on its dining tables shows off much precious metal. My hosts are generous to a traveller, but they suffer the ills of their class, marooned off here in a snowy far corner of the world. They're smug and provincial, preoccupied with their own importance and politics. They scorn, but are eager for the latest of foreign fashions (only the latest!) — which they assiduously imitate while they turn up their noses and sniff, and make superior faces.

I pay off my keep in traveller's currency. That is, I divert my particular table in the dining hall with accounts of my days at the other side of the world, in the warmth of the tropics. The northern wind moans in the big tiled hearth chimney, and between the rows of raised goblets I talk of trade breezes, and palm trees, and the sweet milk of the hairy coconut . . . of seas blue and warm as the midsummer sky, of brown-skinned tribes who idle away their days dressed for Eden, in flowers and scraps of leaves.

Later, in the smoky common room, after a few hands of badly played cards, I hide a yawn and make sure to compliment my host on the singing of his two unmarried nieces. The pair of them beam and pant, all hefty pink cheeks and ornate braids beside the spinet of their music instructor. I even find a moment or two for my brand of commerce, involving some articles of dubious exotic provenance carried with me discreetly in my luggage.

It's all quite tedious and familiar, this traveller's sojourn, apart from the vast snows, and the imperious cold, and the peculiar, gleaming antiquity of the onion domes. But it happens I'm grateful for the storm and its delays. It brings me

a romantic dalliance, which I pursue at first with amusement; and then, to my traveller's surprise, with genuine agitated passion.

On the first night of snow, I hurry along an outer
gallery, on the way back to my room. It's a not-much-
travelled course, a route I've never used before, but I'm concerned about the bodings of the weather, and want to gauge
them firsthand. I see ahead a young woman under one of
the massive ancient stone arches. Clad in silvery fur she is
laughing at the swirling snowflakes, her hands out to catch
them, her face thrust up. I approach slowly and look on,
amused. I tremble under my several traveller's shawls from
the cold. Suddenly this wintry bacchante spins around. She
regards me, startled. I smile at her. All at once she laughs
again, and spins back about, and resumes her enjoyments.

"So you like the snow," I declare, grinning, and quite
charmed by the glimpse of her I've just had. She only
laughs. I don't remember seeing her before, and the nature
of her cone-topped hat, and the old-style shaggy verve of
her coat, are ambiguous as to her status. She could be a
friend of the household. She could still be one of the staff.
I demand her name, but she won't respond. I watch the
flakes whirling down around her. She collects a gloveful and
merrily licks it. I laugh myself, shaking my head. "You
strange northern folk!" I tease. This remark makes her mer-
rier. Abruptly she turns, and thrusts the catch of snow toward me for a taste. I take the traveller's liberty and seize
her wrist playfully, and tug to press in for a kiss. She pushes
me off. "Now now —" she rebukes. She laughs in high spirits and pirouettes slowly away, face and hands up to the nonstop snow.

"I must go in," I announce, beguiled and a little

perplexed. "Or I'll catch my death out here! But I can tell I won't be travelling in this weather," I go on. "Where and when can I see you again? In more comfortable surroundings," I add.

I pass the night on my heaped pillows, under the blankets and rugs, my dreams spiced by a curious girl in a conical hat ringed with fur — a pale girl with lovely grey eyes, slanted in the northern manner and slightly weak, and a small laughing mouth, and round white pretty cheeks.

She meets me every violent night of the epic storm, but always in that outer gallery. The stealthy comforts of my room, or the secluded warmth of a back hallway I've employed a couple of times for amorous matters, she refuses. I learn to dress in proper furry fashion for our snowy assignations. No one ever surprises us as we loiter there conversing under a guttering taper, or wander up and down as the wind flails and lashes, while she recites to me stories of the old capital and its winters. She sings me songs that have been written through the years in their honor. Then she laughs, and she springs away and I watch her salute the turbulent flurries with joyous arms. When she turns to me, gleeful and spattered with flakes, I sweep her up in my bulky arms, and she lets me briefly taste her lips, lips so cold and tantalizing. But never anything more — this curious, bewitching acolyte of the north.

I in my turn offer up the lures of the tropics, but I have to say she seems indifferent about them, to my slightly offended amusement. "My rabbit," I call her, for her pretty plumpness in her silvery fur. "My snow rabbit," because of the rare whiteness of her cheeks. Sometimes she looks so pale I tease her that I fear how long she is for this world. I confess this with a mock catch in my voice, and a sigh, which provokes her laugh. But my mockery has a tender edge to it. I bring her rum, bottled in the Indies, to build up her color; but she dislikes the taste. I make a present of the dried husk of an orange, plucked oceans away in the equator's heat. I scratch my name across this dusky reliquary globe, with a pang at the gesture's evocations. She sniffs it for a moment. The one gift she takes to heart is a sprig of coral, wrenched from a South Seas floor, which resembles, she decides, a fossil of sprouted ice. I scheme up presents to sway a girl in love with the snows of winter, while my lusters as a guest grow dulled, my charts and calibrations sit neglected.

Then the tumultuous skies exhaust themselves. The old capital lies transfixed in its drifts. That night, when she appears, my friend seems strangely agitated, distracted. I've ceased to press her on where she comes from, how she manages to make her way here every time through such a turbulent universe. She's not herself now. She barely acknowledges the new gift I uncover in my hand, as she stands staring out at the icy, hushed darkness. She ends our rendezvous early — abruptly. All at once I turn into the truest of lovers: I fear the worst. My heart won't let me sleep, there in the piled disorder of my bed.

The next night, for the first time, she's late. When she appears she ignores my protests. She seems more agitated than before, shockingly pale in her silvery furs. Her eyes glitter. "Would you like to come with me tonight?" she exclaims suddenly, gripping my hand. My heart leaps. "Oh my dearest love —" I tell her wildly. I kiss her but then she pushes me away. "We should hurry," she insists.

We pass undetected out into the street. The snow no longer drains the heavens, but the wind has revived. It

beleaguers the old city, it swirls blinding eddies in the air.
"Shall I hail a sleigh?" I ask, descrying a few late ones still
out prowling for revelers. "No, no, it's not far," she says hurriedly. She leads me plodding off, my hand in her grip. We
bend low as the wind rakes over us. We turn laboriously
from the main thoroughfare, and then down along a suddenly mean lesser route, with decrepit wooden hovels and
then open wastes. I exclaim in protest, and after the snow
grows deeper and the night blacker, I exclaim again. The
wind hurls the snow in stinging billows. I begin to shiver
and sweat in my coat. "Where are we?" I not so much ask
as demand. We've halted. She releases my hand from her
grasp. "We're here," she replies.

I peer about in confusion. I blink at her under the icy
brim of my hat. "Here?" I repeat stupidly, seeing no grand
buildings, no little houses, only wastes of snow, tormented
by the wind. "My darling," she proclaims. I stare at her in
horror . . . at the unearthly pallor of her plump flesh. She
throws off her cone-shaped hat, exposing the turbulence of
her hair. "My darling!" she cries, as her coat falls away. Bare
arms reach toward me, to catch me to her. I gasp, and stagger back, transfixed as if in a terrifying dream. "Now I understand," I stammer, hearing my words twisted and shorn
by the wind. "You're not a live thing — you're a ghost! You
are, aren't you —" I exclaim, shuddering in powerless horror. She advances on me, laughing in intimate glittery las-
civiousness. Slowly I stagger back from her, spellbound as I
slowly sink down into the numbing embrace of the snow
drifts. I feel her hands reaching under my coat . . . her stooping mouth closing on mine. I taste the ice of her lips.

It's the curses of a sleigh driver that save me. A sleigh
driver who's lost his way, and disrupts the very wind and

cold with his fury. I struggle, and heave the ghost away from
me, a white figure subsiding back clawing into the tormented whiteness. I flounder off toward the shouts and
whipcracks, screaming for my life.

My hosts tend me solicitously. Nobly even. They move
me to a more lavish bedroom, and call in their personal
physician, aided by the two unmarried nieces, to supervise
my recuperation. This consists chiefly in keeping me warm,
if not hot; of surrounding me in a furry cocoon and lacing
my medicinal broth with my own rum. The hospitable so-
licitude touches me deeply, as does the discretion in not in-
quiring how I came to be in such a place, in such a state, in
the middle of such a night. It crosses my mind that as na-
tives of the old city and its winters, my hosts might in fact
possess some wisdom about a jaded traveller's unexpected
gullibilities. Especially those of the heart. . . .

When I take my leave, I present them all with some of
the rarer souvenirs and relics from my tropical cache. The
best of course I still keep with me, packed away religiously
in my luggage, with me in fact right under the furs and
shawls and carpets of my sleigh. I wave a gloved farewell.
The unmarried nieces weep, the foul-tongued driver brandishes his great whip to get us off. And I depart the old
northern capital, skimming over its imperious snows past
the onion domes and the tiled spires, the oddly pastel splendors, and then turning, to set my course for the truer em-
braces of the south.

Pouches

POUCHES

The scout comes running back toward us shouting, his loincloth bobbing, his jostling spear flashing in the sunlight. My native guide hears his news in its breathless torrent of clucks and gibberish. He chews somberly on his bottom lip. "Well?" I demand. We're about to emerge, I am informed, into a country where precautions have now to be taken. To assuage aroused spirits; to assure them we intend no aggression.

The guide steps past me and sharply issues orders to the bearers. They set down their loads, murmuring. Glancing at each other, they open their mouths gaping wide. They reach in and start removing their teeth. They stow the gleaming items into the pouches among the beads around their necks. I watch in suspicious distaste. The guide returns to my side. "You too, *bwana*," he informs me, his mouth shrunken like an old man's. I hold myself stiffly upright. "I absolutely shall not," I reply, hearing the starchy ring of my voice. "It's beneath my dignity, as a civilized man," I declare. The guide starts to protest. I cut him off with a sharp motion of my hand. "Let's get moving, shall we?" I tell him. He looks at me. He grunts. He tugs his pouch straight and turns on his bare heel and exhorts the bearers once more to their burdens.

Amid this strange company, I enter a dry flatland of

high, sun-scorched grass. Every few hundred yards a
twisted plane tree rises up, like a piece of abandoned sculp-
ture. We make camp. The bearers eat mush and giggle away
at each other's countenances. But their eyes are hard and
fearful. The guide intrudes on my tent, apologizing, while
I'm still laboring over the boiled meat of my dinner. Again
he makes his plea; again I dismiss it. "You ought to see yourself in the mirror, *granddad*," I joke roughly. He retires, his
earring disk waggling as he shakes his head at the consequences.

In the middle of the night, I wake up to a low growling
outside my tent. I stab a hand about for my gun, and sit up
holding it at my side, pointing uncertainly at the tent wall.
A roar goes up that makes my hair stand on end. I tilt back
in mesmerized fright, my finger slowly closing on the trigger. Another roar. The gun blast tears a hole into the tent,
into the vast night itself. A voice screams. General clamor.
The noise of running. The guide bursts into my tent. One
of the bearers has been almost carried off by a beast! All because I still insist on my teeth, he cries, shrivel-mouthed
against starlight at my tent flap. "Nonsense, nonsense," I retort, shaken. I fumble with my canvas bag, for the whiskey
flask. "Someone must have left food out, the animal smelled
it," I insist. "Get the medicine, fix the man's wounds," I go
on. I gulp an agitated swallow that spills down my chin.

The next morning we set off with the injured man tottering along on a makeshift crutch, supported by someone's
shoulder. The extra work for the other bearers slows us
down. I brood, feeling the sullenness of pursed mouths
around me. The sidelong glances. I'm all too aware of the
dire consequences of a mutiny, out here in such circumstances. At lunchtime, I decide I have no other choice. I call

the guide over. His face lights up in relief. He leads me behind the privacy of a plane tree and shows me how it's done.
I stop him after my uppers are out. "That's enough.
Enough," I tell him. My speech whistles thick and broad,
like a six-year-old's after a playground mishap. The guide
counters in alarm that everything must be removed, for the
proper observance of diplomacy. "No, no, this is fine, as a
symbolic gesture of supplication," I exclaim. "Believe me,"
I assure him, "I understand about all this animistic hocus-
pocus. Believe me." I order him back to his charges.

But it's vanity that's playing my hand in this. And a
stubborn pride of culture that's feeling offended.

"You know, I do this for your sake," I inform the guide,
as I rejoin our party. I sniff pointedly. "I myself trust in this,
and this," I declare, tapping my head under my bush hat,
and then my gun in its holster. "Now tell them all to stop
grumbling like that," I order. "And let's get back on the
trail."

During the night there's another attack. At light of day
my tent is riddled with bullet holes, scorched with gun-
smoke. I realize the intolerable: I will have to fully submit.
My cheeks throb scarlet when the guide is done assisting
me. I lift my trembling chin as high as it will go. "Kindly
remove the shaving mirror from my tent," I announce, my
gums clanging strangely, "and have it hidden from my
sight. And do not break it, thank you," I add.

We resume. Through the long stunned hours of heat
and plodding silence, I seem to make out one tiny sound: the
high distinct clinking of our pouches. The night passes,
tense but undisturbed. The following one too. The guide
can't restrain a small crumpled smile of triumph as he sees
me at my plate of mush. I ignore him.

On the last of these days, to my mortification, we encounter a party headed the other way. My bush-jacketed
equal greets me with firm-mouthed cheerful courtesy, with
barely a hitch in his manner at my condition. But the
briefest narrowing of his pale eyes gives away his private
thoughts: that one of his kind has degraded himself, has
soiled his cultural authority by submitting to the grotes-
queries of savages. I stare off into the grass, mumbling commonplaces through the screen of my hand. I ask the loan of
some medicines for our injured. These are supplied with patronizing generosity. We salute good-bye. "You'll learn,
sonny boy," I mutter clacking, watching the upright proud
pale back moving off. "I will be clear of here tomorrow
morning, and reassembled," I go on. "You, in your foolish,
starched pride, have terrors and horrors awaiting you."

I turn, and my guide falls in beside me. "He, in his foolish arrogant pride, has terrors and horrors awaiting him,"
he declares. I glance at him sharply. I shrug. I stare ahead.
"Whether or not that is so, that is no business of yours," I
inform him, to reclaim the order of things. And the next
day, mercifully, we leave the angry grasslands; we open up
our pouches, and after some fumbling, all goes back to
proper order. Except for the guide's lingering trace of a
smile, which, of course, I ignore.

GIBBET

I'm on my way to meet a sorcerer. In the midst of my journey, I reach a famous town and its oasis. There, under orange and yellow awnings of the marketplace, sellers tend
with whisks their piled fruits and vegetables. Others pull at
the sleeves of their robes and bark at the traveller idling
along, about the wonders of their rabbits and pullets. Or the
heaped splendors of their carpets and rugs. I lift back the
corner of one, to admire its silky woven traceries. Then I
turn my head and wander off toward a hubbub.

The stark angle of a gibbet rises against the harsh blue
sky. A thief is about to be hanged. In this case the culprit is
a monkey, being punished for stealing fruit. The creature
makes a farce of his end, to the jeers of the crowd. In his
little red fez he falls to his knees uncooperatively on the
scaffold, screeching pathetically for mercy, showing off his
big abject monkey teeth and gums, his paws lashed behind
above his tail, the noose already around his neck. The two
hangmen in the balloon trousers of their trade cuff him and
kick at him to rise. The monkey ducks and bobs. Someone
beside me throws a mocking chunk of gory watermelon.
More follow. One of the missiles strikes a hangman. Then
his partner. Annoyed, the two of them rebuke the crowd. A
hail of fruit splatters the scaffold. The hangmen draw their
scimitars and brandish them.

In the distraction the monkey sees his chance. With

hectic dexterity, he flips into the air and grabs on to the rope
above him by his feet, and with the aid of his sinuous tail
he starts hauling himself aloft upside down. The hangmen
rush over and mill underneath, roaring. The crowd cheers
the frenzied acrobat on, my own voice among theirs. At the
top of the gibbet, the monkey wriggles his bound paws to
the front and wrenches free of the noose, knocking his fez
off. It tumbles jaunty and red to the scaffold, as the monkey
hops up and down screeching in triumph. Then he turns
and raises his tail and lets loose a stream of filth. General
uproar. An arrow whistles past the monkey. A second thuds
into the wood by his feet. Soldiers muscle through the crowd
with their bows and quivers.

The monkey darts from side to side along the gibbet's
branch in a final reckless display of exultation. Then he
springs out onto a yellow awning and, astoundingly, up to
the tiles of a roof. Cheers and whistles. An arrow blooms out
of his rump. He squawks, and clambers on ludicrously, and
disappears yelping over the rooftop. The arrow shaft sticks
upright for a moment against the blazing blue, to laughter
all around. I drift off through the jabbering throngs, smiling to myself and shaking my head. All at once I stagger,
from a shoulder. A turbaned soldier jolts me aside as he
rushes on past in pursuit of the escapee. He throws me an
implacable glance. The arrow feathers jar and rattle above
the lip of his quiver. I stoop to retrieve my fallen new cap
and deliberately bang off the dust before I fit it back on my
head. I continue on my way, after first checking about for
any more oncoming imperious arms of the law.

I refresh my dignity in a food shop with a plate of yo-
gurt and figs. I watch soldiers thud along past the window
gratings, shouting orders. Eventually I make my way back
to where I'm lodging. More soldiers here, stalking through

the wide arches of the portico, in and out of light and shade, after their quarry. A sullen, turbaned stare follows me to the threshold of my room. Its source thumps with his fist on a door a distance away.

I grunt sourly and go in. Frowning, I remove my cap, and flicking at a trace of dirt still there, I carry it across to the clothes cupboard. I stow it on the shelf with deliberate care, setting the bill just so. Then I flinch. A fetid, alien odor reaches my nostrils. I curse in disgust and puzzlement. I sniff. It seems to rise from the depths of the cupboard. Grimacing I shove through the flimsy welter of robes and ornamented bags. Suddenly, in a jolt of surprise, I gasp. A small, immensely hairy hand closes on my wrist. Beyond it, dirty warm brown eyes stare up at me from the dimness. I stare back, assailed by the odor.

There's a thumping at my door. I swing my head toward it. The little hand squeezes tighter. I turn back. The felonious monkey tilts his dark muzzle and implores me in desperate silence with a big gummy grin of abjection distorting his wide lips. There's a frozen pause: I stand at the mouth of the reeking cupboard, held there by the beseeching clasp on my wrist. A clasp begging the fellowship of those roughly treated by authority. A clasp invoking the tradition of empathy for the underdog. A clasp that issues, I realize all at once, from my new silk blouse, now stained with animal foulness and dark blood. The thumping at the door redoubles. "Open up!" demands a sullen voice. "Come in!" I shout, and I wrench my arm free, and step away backward into the room.

A pair of soldiers come stalking in. I jerk my head toward the hiding place. They draw their curved daggers. The capture is over after a brief, ugly struggle. The battered monkey is dragged away for his gibbet slung on the frame of two spears, moaning from the blows and the horrendous dislocation of a shoulder. He still has on part of my ruined shirt. His brown eyes fix on me in accusation for my treachery, my transgression against fellowship. I lean sullenly against a wall, staring at the tiled floor.

I pass a troubled night, the air oppressive and close. Lightning flickers through the lattices of the window grating without the release of rain. I decide on my sleepless pillow to press on toward my journey's goal, and in the morning I settle my bill and carry my bags over to the stable. My horse has not been well cared for, I discover, and I quarrel with the stable owner. I start out toward the desert. The sky hangs close, ominous and dim as we pick our way to the first dunes over the outlying hills. My horse shies so often, I have to walk him a while. I remount and go on cautiously. The doings of yesterday sit uneasily with me. It's no light thing for a traveller to transgress abiding conventions of succor, and I have to goad myself to attend what lies ahead, the business of my journey, which will require great care and caution. Wise about hidden things, the sorcerer is a notoriously dangerous and provocative character, prone to unexpected disguises, impersonations. Strange strategies involving omens. A thought suddenly grips me by the throat.

I wrench the reins. My horse writhes frantically and rears up, flailing with his hooves. We wheel around and around chaotically in the dust, until I can bring him under control. Crying out, I dig my spurs in his flanks and lash him with the trails of the reins, left and right. Desperately we gallop off back toward the distant spires of the town, where the dark angle of the gibbet rises like the half-opened knife of my fate.

CANTINA

I go into a cantina in the jungle. It's not much more than a shed with a plank bar and a few tables. I settle myself at one of the tables and open my bag and spread out my charts. I scrutinize distances, durations. The light falls badly for this sort of work. I look around at the lamp overhead and wrench my table closer to it. From the bar the proprietor calls out in protest. I shrug at him and gesture, appealing to his understanding. He regards me fixedly. I roll my eyes to myself, and move the table back a little toward where it was, in submission to protocol, his authority in his place. Pursing my lips I squint again over my charts. Behind me the voices of a couple of other drinkers in the place grow agitated. A fight threatens. I glance around over my shoulder in annoyance a moment, and continue my calculations. Finally I roll the charts up and put them back in my bag and sit with my drink.

A man also with a bag comes walking over and calmly sits down at my table, without asking. I blink stolidly at him. He grins. He wears a hat that was dandyish long ago, in its pristine state. "How nice to see a man of intelligence, who can use his mind, in this part of the world," he says. "Maps," he declares, with a suggestive grin. I look down slowly and regard my bag, at which he's pointing. I look back at him. "Oh, those are all just for show," I tell him evenly. "None of

the configurations have the slightest accuracy or applica-
tion. I just like to bring them out in places like this, to im-
press the locals," I declare.

He looks back at me. Then he laughs, with exaggerated
ease. He wipes at his long, weathered neck with a drab
handkerchief. "Well now, I myself have something a man
like you would be interested in," he says. "If you will just
step outside, I'll show you. You can judge for yourself." I regard him. After a longish moment, I shrug. "As you please,"
I tell him.

"All right," I declare, when we've gone out onto the log-
ging track twenty or thirty yards. I keep the lighted mouth
of the cantina clearly in view. I have my bag tightly in hand.
Insects throb in the fleshy blades of the walls of vegetation.
An overripe moon hangs low, in a swarm of swollen stars.
The would-be vendor nods to me, an unlit cheroot in his
teeth. He sets down his bag and squats and opens it, and
stands back up with the gauze-wrapped object he's brought
out. He grins under his grimy, dented hat, crudely enjoying
the salesman-like suspense. I scowl at him, at what he has
in his hand. He begins to unravel it. My heart for its reasons
begins to quiver. The hair rises on the back of my neck. The
darkness pulses around us. The man unspools the wrapping,
meridian after meridian, fixing me with his door-to-door
grin. As the round mass in his hands grows smaller, he
grunts gleefully under his breath, seeing me staring. Finally
he wrenches streamers of wrapping into the air. His sup-
porting hand is empty. "What? —" I exclaim dumbly. He
throws back his hatted head and pulls clear his cheroot and
yelps with laughter. "Sorry, sorry, friend," he cries, delighted. "All a gag. Having you on!" He puts out a hand to
my shoulder, to press it solicitously, but I push him away.

Sputtering, I call him a name. I'm red in the face, outraged, confused. "Oh come on!" he laughs, as I shove past him and head back into the cantina.

I sit at the table, furious. The proprietor looks over at me a couple of times. He signals to me. "What is it?" I demand shortly. "You are upset, mister," he says. I give a bark of unamused laughter, at the semidelicacy of this question, considering my surroundings. "I'm *annoyed*," I inform him. "Like anyone, I don't enjoy being made a fool of." He nods somberly. A flicker of a smirk plays over his lips. I grunt sourly at it, and go back to my drink. A while later the joker in the hat drifts back in from the darkness with his bag. The wrapping hangs from his jacket pocket, where he's stuffed it. He looks my way with disingenuous, mocking apology, cheroot waggling in his teeth. I rub my chin and work my lips and turn away. I cross my legs. I look at my watch. There are still several hours to go before dawn, before my newest appointment and its familiar gravities, its heart-wrenching promises. I twist the heel of my glass on the table. I rub my face. I edge my bag of precious charts closer in under my leg. At the planked bar, Mr. Hi-Jinx, hat shoved back, and the proprietor lounge together over a bottle. They grin across my way. Nonplussed, I stare out beyond them; the blackness of the monstrous night frames them, looming.

BY THE PATH

I lead the native pony down to the stream. I pull off a couple of saddlebags to ease his load, and stand watching as he drinks. The sound of his lapping fills the stillness between the banks and rises into the trees. He lifts a back hoof and lowers it, as he gives his head a shake. I heft the bags and take a step toward him, to clear away his sweat. Then I halt. I turn just my head, slowly, and look back up at the rim of the bank behind me. I let the saddlebags go to the ground. I raise my hands uncertainly. I turn about fully toward the bank, staring up at the figure of a girl watching from above. She trains a gun on me.

"What're you doing here?" she demands.

I make a small gesture, keeping my hands aloft. I regard her sideways. "I'm just passing through," I answer. "On my way somewhere, from somewhere else." There's silence after this unadorned declaration. The girl's brow narrows, wary and puzzled. I smile in careful amusement. The cut of her jacket, once naively plush and jaunty, is now stained and torn from its circumstances. "If you don't mind, I'm going to lower my hands," I tell her. "And I really would prefer if you found somewhere else to point that weapon." "Why should I?" she replies. "Because," I inform her, my hands descending, "I bring no harm with me, for anyone." I smile again, looking calmly back at her. Silence again. I let it go on. The pony peers around at us from the stream. "Listen —" I begin finally, but she interrupts. "Well, someone means harm around here," she says. I tilt my head. "What do you mean?" I tell her. "Come up here," she says, after a pause. "Very slowly."

I stare down, scowling, at the body lying half-hidden among the flowers and foliage at the side of the path. "How could I have missed it?" I mutter to myself. "Do you know who he is?" the girl says. I shake my head, noting the ashen cheek, the buckled, bloodied hat. "Are you sure?" she presses. I direct a hard, silent look at her. I gaze again down at the body, and then go in and kneel over it, for a closer examination among the nodding blossoms.

I come back to the girl grimly. "We shouldn't stay around here," I tell her. "We'd better travel together until we're in different country." I gaze back along the path, where her pony waits. I cross in front of her, to get down to the stream. "How come you didn't notice him?" she demands nervously. She takes a step after me. "How come — answer me!" she cries. I stop, halfway down the bank, and peer back up. She has the weapon raised again. I regard her, exasperated. "Because I had my mind on other things," I inform her. "What other things?" she demands. "Listen," I demand in return, "have I asked you what you're doing here? Have I?" I turn away and head toward the pony. "I suggest you hurry and get down here," I call back, without looking. "Unless you want to wind up there beside him after nightfall."

We cross the stream and start into the lush woods beyond, forcing the pace. When the light fades, there's not enough moon to go by, and we have to make camp. We eat without a fire and lie side by side in our blankets, with the ponies tethered close by. I have my own weapon with me, from my saddlebags. I stare into the implacable darkness.

"We're far enough," I murmur, listening to the night sounds. "We should be all right. . . ." The girl makes a whimper of almost childish concern beside me. It makes me turn and smile at her. She has a scarf's grimy sheen tucked up to her ears, against the night air. "I wish I could trust you more," she complains. "I just don't see how you could have missed —" "Here we go again," I interrupt her. I swing my head from side to side and squeeze my eyes shut for a moment, in disbelief and annoyance. I look at her. "I told you," I insist. "I told you, I was preoccupied with other concerns. . . ." The girl isn't assured. "How long have you been out here," she wants to know, distressed. "How long have you been?" I retort. "A few months," she says. Her voice quavers. "Four or five. I've started to lose track." "I'm that in years," I inform her. I lean close. "Look, I've seen enough like that back there to last me amply for a lifetime," I declare. "I know exactly what to do." "What?" she asks. I answer slowly and with savage emphasis. "Get the hell from it as far as possible," I tell her.

I turn away. I stare into the darkness. The ponies are quiet. They'll function as our alarms. "Why'd you come out here?" I ask the girl, not looking. "Searching for a lost parent, a loved one?" "Yes," she replies faintly beside me. "How did you know?" Her tone is startled. "That's what brought us all to these godforsaken places," I reply. "At least in the beginning. Trying to reclaim our hearts." There's a pause. "Do you still have any hope?" I ask quietly. The girl doesn't answer right away. I realize she's sobbing. "Oh god," she wails softly, her small shoulders quaking under the blanket, her weapon trembling in her hands. "Oh dear god. . . ."

BREAK-IN

I come back to my room at the hotel after supper. Someone has broken in. My suitcase has been forced open. All my maps have been switched with other, useless ones.

I go downstairs at once and ring for the night manager. "I shall go and notify the authorities immediately," he says. He turns briskly from the counter and walks straight into a wall. "Damn it," he exclaims, rubbing his nose. "They must have broken in here too when I was in back. They've moved the wall. But don't you worry," he declares. He waves a re-assuring, admonitory finger. "They won't get away with it!" "I'm over here," I mutter. "What's that?" he asks, looking about. "There you are," he says. He feels his way along the counter toward the alcove which contains the phone.

I thrust my hands in my pockets and wander back upstairs, hearing the laborious conversation behind me. "Police? No, no, I'm not the police, you're the police! PO—LICE, I say. What? Speak up, I can't hear you! I say I can't —" I reach my room finally and close the door on all this uselessness. I sit, mulling over the futile bounty of deliberately wrong charts and topographical renderings pitched around me on the floor. I take one up and try to distract my anxiety with speculations:

Suppose I was indeed bound for this city so elaborately recorded in my hand. Which road would I take? This one, by a river? Or this, along the rim of a mountainside? Where would I stay: here, in this wayside? Or there, in that curiously named village. How would the names of these places pair with the actual look, the experience, the memory of them? What would spring to mind, years on, when such and such a name repeated itself to me? I idle, imagining. . . . Luckily, I try to reassure myself, I marked things on the real maps in haphazard code. But then one can't be certain — doesn't know whom one's dealing with in break-ins like this. My ease is now once more spoiled, and I toss the replacement map away and stretch out on the bed, brooding somberly.

Someone comes tapping along the corridor outside. Finally there's a knock on my door. It's the idiot of a night manager. The police will be here shortly, he thinks. He laughs awkwardly. "I'm sorry," he exclaims, "but I can't recall exactly why it was they should be called. Would you mind refreshing my memory!" I look at him. I start to answer, but then I think the better of it. "I have to say I don't know what you're talking about," I tell him. "And if I did, it's slipped my mind. Now I'm very sorry myself, but I'm turning in now," I announce. "I must be off early to resume my journey." I shut the door on his perplexity, and my lies. I'll be off at dawn, that much is true. But it will now be an odd, sham journey, as I have only patently false versions of where I go.

Interruption

INTERRUPTION

I bend over my pencil at the table, scratching away at fancies and fabrications. Suddenly I'm aware I'm not alone. I twist around.

A gaunt figure stands cravenly by the threshold. Thinning grey hair hangs around its ears, and shadows etch its eyes. It more or less wrings its hands in apology and discomfort. Dingy clothes droop over its frame, a few degrees above rags.

It's my inner self.

"What the hell —" I demand.

"I'm sorry, I'm sorry," it stammers. "I just —"

"You just *what?*" I interrupt.

"I just — got lonely," it announces, squirming, its voice trailing away.

I look at it. I snort. I turn back to the table. "Well, I don't know, go see a movie," I inform it over my shoulder. "Or ride on the subway. I need another hour here, at least. I can't work," I exclaim, "as you very well know, with you lurking around."

I start to sharpen my pencil. But I don't hear the door close. I swing my head back, with a glare of incredulity. The figure shifts in distress from foot to foot, the very image of pained anxiety, of neurotic purpose.

"What *is* it?" I mutter, in savage, exasperated intimacy.

"You can't wait another goddam hour to get in here and masturbate?"

Such a jolt of pain clamors across its grey visage at this that I immediately hold up a hand in apology. I sigh. I lay my pencil down deliberately on the table. "All right," I address it, massaging my temples, glancing at the clock as it ticks away at the afternoon. "Go ahead, what's the problem?"

There's more of the preliminary stammering, the shifting of moth-eaten shoes. "It's just," I hear, "it's just — I've been, you know — and don't be mad at me — reading some of what you've written — and —" My out-thrust hand cuts off the sentence.

"You've been reading my stuff!" I snarl.

"Well, yes, I mean — I mean — well of course I have," the figure blurts hotly, all atremble. "Why the hell shouldn't I, it's all about me!"

I stare at it. "All right, all right," I mutter. "Don't squeak."

"I'm not squeaking," it retorts. "Yes you are," I murmur under my breath. "Squeak, squeak."

"It's just — just —" the figure stammers on, looking as if it were running in place now, it's squirming so. "It's just — I mean, well how come you never write about the real me? How come I always have to be in some far-off place, suffering, you know, weird travails, decked out in goofy costumes? Guilty of horrible crimes that aren't even clearly named!" It blinks its dimming eyes at me, and its voice turns positively shrill. "How come it's never just me as I really and truly am? How come?" it demands.

And it stares at me, chin jutting in grievance, in pleading defiance.

I stare back in silence, grimly. I work my lips, deeply inflamed. My instinct of imagination has been impugned, which I refuse to tolerate.

"Because," I reply, slowly. "In that case, no one would be interested. Or entertained."

The face before me trembles. "What'd'ya mean?" it says.

"I mean," I snap, "what's there about the real you to write about?"

This produces a veritable tremor of dismay. "What'd'ya mean?" the impulse threatens, once again; but mercifully, variety intervenes. "That's not true," the figure insists. "Lots!" it adds. There's a sulky, wounded pause. "Lots," it murmurs.

"Oh," I reply, ruthless. "You mean how you're aging? And poor? And obscure? And waste so many hours playing with yourself that I practically have to use a stun gun on you, to clear you out of here long enough for me to get some work done? Is that what you mean?" I press on, witheringly. "Or is it your corrosive loneliness?" I wonder. "Or perhaps your swollen egotism and craven insecurity? Not to mention your crippling jealousies, your nonstop self-loathing? And your dingy clothes? And the pseudo-artsy poke-hole, stuck away here high among old office buildings, where you groan awake to every light of day, to start waiting for the phone to ring?

"Is that what you mean?" I snarl.

There's harrowed silence when I'm done. The grey head sags in the dimness. The shadows around the grey figure are like ruins.

I realize I've gone too far, overstepped propriety, regardless of the intimacy of our relations. I rub at my forehead in troubled exasperation. I take a long breath. I struggle up and go over to the trembly figure. I put my arm around it and chafe its wilted sleeve.

"Hey there," I murmur. "Hey, forgive me, I spoke a lot of cranky crap!" A grey finger swipes at the drop of moisture hanging off the long nose. "And I'm not ashamed of you at all, if that's what you're thinking. But you understand?" I go on softly. "It's just that people like things dressed up. They don't want to hear about some regular Joe and his woes in a poky room somewhere. They want to be carried away — they want steamy jungles, gunshots, ghosts and corpses, disasters up in mountain snows! Romance, adventure, grotesquery!" I give its shoulder a jostle, to buck it up. "Readers are like kids, they like their heroes running around in funny outfits. You know that, you old coot!" I tease. "They like you in a pith helmet, or a purple cloak! Or a sombrero!" I jostle it again. Finally it nods, its lower lip stuck out in emotion.

"I know — I mean, it's just — it's just —" it stammers, as ever.

I sigh. I glance at the clock, and its losses.

"Alright, how's this?" I bargain. "Here's five bucks that was going to go for beer later, go on down and treat yourself to a big decaffeinated cappuccino at the new bookstore and read a couple of magazines for a few extra minutes. Let me get on with my business here," I propose, "and when I'm done I'll throw in an extra item, just for you, just the way you'd like it: You As You Really Are."

It turns its haggard face to me. Its rimmed eyes are glowing. "You will?" it says.

"I will," I promise. I clap it on the back. "But lay off, please, going over my stuff like that. Okay?" I declare. It nods, biting its lip. Another clap on the back, and I send it shuffling on its way down the corridor to the elevator, carefully clutching the five.

I lock the door with a sarcastic flourish. I turn back into the room, and sigh, and curse precisely, and run a hand through my own scant, but at least tidy, hair. Then I get back to my chair and resume my interrupted transmutation. And then finally, as the clock ticks down, I cram in a few lines to keep my promise, which is what I'm doing right here.

CITYSCAPE

Night has fallen when I haul myself up and over the last couple of metal rungs, and slump onto the safety of the rooftop. For a while I just lie there, rolled onto my big pack and coil of rope on the tar paper. I'm too limp to move. Above me, the stars drift like a faint sea of lights in the high thin overcast. A sky promising rain, again. I grunt, and move my toes reflexively in their red-laced boots, which have not held up so far in foul weather.

Then slowly I sit. I unstrap my helmet and let the night breeze chill my damp head. I feel at the gash in my tweed trouser leg, where the insane woman lunged out at me from her kitchen window, to slash with a knife as I labored past. I blow out a grim sigh, calling to mind other hazards along the way, such as the encounter with two stories of wildly flapping laundry on a fire escape in a hailstorm. Or the attack of the flock of pigeons, and their lethal spoor.

Rubbing my jaw, I recall another, lingering, image, of a few evenings ago . . . an opened curtained window, and from the lamplight beyond, over the low crooning voice of a radio, the intimate cries of a woman, the laboring exclamations of a man. And myself, there in all my gear, pressed against the brick wall stories up outside.

A lone crackpot climber, transfixed in his passage.

I shake my head. I think again of that innocent morn-

ing a week ago, in my narrow little room, when I cinched
the last buckle, hefted my pack, tugged the final strap.
When I threw open the window and clambered through,
and began this idiot's adventure.

I snort to myself. I gaze around, at the apartment blocks
dwindled below, and the soaring promontories of the
office towers I'm perched among, high up here. The grand
edifices of commerce are like cliffs barnacled with air-
conditioners, and honeycombed with a thousand windows,
a few lonely ones still lit like . . . like what? The last re-
maining stars in the cold dark husks of dying ant gal-
axies. . . .

I turn my head from these ruminations, to look for the
building's water tower. Then I stiffen. A door creaks open
in the roof-access hut in the darkness. I unsnap my holster
and step back with my hand on my revolver. A splash of
light falls on the roof in front of me. Foreign voices. Figures
appear. A match flares. A couple of young floor cleaners, up
for a cigarette. When they notice me and my melodramat-
ics, they halt. They mutter to each other, and then retreat
grumbling, slamming the door after them.

I wait, alone again under the night sky. I snap my holster back shut. I check my pack is secure, and then I stiffly
wander over to the water tower on its stilts. I soak a handkerchief in the dribble of overflow and wipe my sweat-stiff
face, and my neck. I probe my tender leg again in the dim
starlight, through the knife damage in my trousers.

After a cold meal from a can, I lift my head to gaze high
beyond the dark bulk of the water tower. The bristling
turrets of a landmark skyscraper loom there, massed cor-
nices and gables and horned buttresses riding the spotlit
heights. I fight through my awe to fix a climber's scrutiny

on the verdigrised slope of the crowning, copper-gilded pyramid . . . on the massive caryatids posed like slave Atlases under the last lofty balconies . . . on the terra-cotta extravaganzas where my footholds and perches and rope tie offs will lie.

I scan the route that will lead me crawling and inching up to the glowing lantern in the cupola at the very top. I look down and curse under my breath, again, at the quality of my boots.

Shaking my head, I turn back to my equipment. My heart flinches in me at the daunting challenge of what rises ahead. I blow out a hard breath. I set my jaw. I pull on my pack and helmet, heft my rope. All around my slight lone oddball figure, the giant bulwarks of the city thrust their metal and stone geometries aloft into the night. I clamber off, deeper and deeper among them, aspiring.

CHIEF

I live in an igloo," I exclaim, "up near the Pole — wrapped in sealskin, and eating blubber! By the weak light of dawn I rise to watch the white demon — the polar bear — hunt from an ice floe at the horizon —"

The man blinks. "You don't say," he says.

"I slouch in a hammock on an Indies shore," I continue, pacing away and then swinging back. "In the iridescent sunset, I call for rum, and scratch myself with a hank of sugarcane, and make a game of counting the stars as they climb — while a black-and-red bird," I declare, "with its flaming yellow-curved beak, squats in the banana leaves above my head —"

The man smiles, a slight, pleasant smile. He nods. "Go on," he says.

A crackle of foam bubbles at the corner of my lips. I take a snagging, agitated breath and stroke my fingers into my hair. "In the cool of the desert night," I murmur, "I wander over windswept dunes! Swaying to my camel's gait, transfixed by far-away ululations from the tents of the oasis . . . the gossamer tinkle of finger cymbals . . . the jingling of ankle bracelets . . . the thud of bare dancing —"

The door opens. The man turns his head. Another man steps in.

"What you find?" says the first man. The second one

shrugs, holding up a bag. "Just a backpack," he says. "Old Boy Scout type. Cheap little camera. Watercolor sketchbook. A diary, couple of entries, nothing in particular. An old pocket atlas, for kids. Very marked up. A rubber ball . . . blue green, with his name scratched on it."

The first man stares at him. He rubs his head. "Take a look at this," he says. "Hey, chief," he calls to me. "Put your hands up there on the window bars. Go on." "Jesus," says the second man, coming over. "What's he got there, a directory?" "Come on, chief," the first man insists. "Put them back up so he can take a look."

The second man stoops and peers close and reads aloud the homemade tattoos.

My left hand: "Rover" "Explorer"
       "Adventurer" "Wanderer"
       "Fancy-free Rambling Man"
       "Poetic Soul".

On my right hand: "Misfit" "Vagrant"
       "Derelict" "Refugee"
       "Wastrel" "Exile"
       "Deviant" "Idler"
       "Vagabond" "Drifter".

He nods slowly when he's finished. He glances at me sidelong, and straightens. He looks over at his partner.

I shift from foot to grimy foot in the blanket they've given me. "All day I tramp the high mountains!" I proclaim in a blaring voice, staring ahead. "Tracking the horned ram in his wintry crags, trailing the snowy eagle to his fierce, icy nest. . . ."

The second man stares at me. He turns his head and regards the first man again. The two of them leave the room, closing the door on my voice. They walk slowly down the corridor.

The second man blows out a long breath. "Jesus —" he says, shaking his head. The first man nods in concord. "Yup . . ." he says. "Where'd you say they found him again?" asks the second man. "In a broom closet, one flight up, on the ninth floor," answers his partner. "The night watchman heard him. God knows how long he'd been in there. Dressed like that." The second man closes his eyes and slowly shakes his head again. "So what are we going to do with him?" he says. The first man scratches his cheek and grins quietly, in pain. "You always ask the easy questions," he says.

They turn a corner.

Back where they left me, I sit huddled on a windowsill, breathing hard, my head inclined against the bars of the window. Beyond me and around me, the towers of the night city rise, like the dark shoulders of behemoths crowded into a monstrous holding pen. I rock back and forth on my sill, grinning at their epic desolations, my eyes glazed with starlight, with the pale sheen of their thousand mute, late-lit windows.

PREAMBLE

I'm marooned, after an act of foolishness. I've crash-landed on a godforsaken scrap of isle. A few ragtag palms preside over a marshy lump in the ocean's quaking immensity. I'm primordially alone. It's like a joke — a horrible joke on me. I have to laugh, trembling and unshaven under my stained straw hat that still sports the name of a resort hotel. The resort hotel from which, in a drunken midnight grab for a free "extra" of festivity, I stole off in their hot air balloon. For a whirl, whereupon a gale promptly swept me out to sea, and kept sweeping me, screaming and clutching in elemental terror. Until after days and nights I was spewed violently from the clouds onto this seagirt marsh.

The balloon lies there like a great torn sack full of saline muck. Its half-smashed emblazoned basket is my upside-down — what, cradle? I feel sunk that far back before the terrible edifice of the world, and my fate. At night I dwindle to a whimpering dark speck beneath the glittering behemoths of the constellations. By day I enact a young boy's adventurous meager self-reliances. I fish with hook and line from the balloon's survival kit. I catch crabs, swearing, in the slosh of the most marshy places. I hack down coconuts from the trees, using the survival knife, and lap rainwater straight from the survival-kit box upturned as catch basin, eschewing the niceties of the plastic drinking bottle. Now and then I fiddle desperately with the gadget supposed to send out a radio beam bleating far and wide. But it's corroded and inert: a metal rock. At times I just stop in the middle of the noise of all these activities. I just stop, all of a sudden supremely dislocated, and hear the ocean waves in my ears. I throw back my straw-hatted head, and I scream, in my terrified loneliness. I writhe to my feet. "Where are they?" I shriek, arms outstretched to the oblivion of empty sky. "Where are the search planes! *Where are they?*" But clearly I've been forgotten; or simply, ignored. I sink to my knees, gurgling, clawing at my face in anguish.

I feel myself readying for a profound spiritual realignment because of my circumstances. I pace my sandy, marshy purlieus at twilight, somberly, waiting for epiphanies and illuminations. But all I come up with is a brooding, unredeemed cynicism about what's happened to me, a flippant but deep-stained resentment over how things have worked out. A big, nasty grudge that just grows nastier.

One day, out of the ocean's limitlessness, a green bottle washes up. I stare at it in my hands. It's rudely but obsessively corked, and its interior is crammed with what appear to be pages. I smash the vessel on a palm with a trembling heart. Feverishly I devour every close-scribbled, mold-mottled leaf the sea has thrown up to me. They're from the hand of a poor soul in the same straits I am, brought there by a mishap in travel. But obviously he's made far more spiritual hay than I have from the wastes of his extremity. After the obligatory preamble — pleading for rescue, offering vital particulars — he launches into an eloquent, magical testament of a life, both a narrative and hallucination, rich with philosophy that's distilled from rumination and fancy and the vantage of isolation.

He sees his role in life to have been, in its essence, a traveller — a haunted traveller. What haunted him? Fate? His losses of the heart? His own private self? He travelled to probe the answer to this question: a travel in a circle. His journeys traversed the internal as well as the grand outer world. The imaginary as well as the actual. He adopted guises unconstrained, he inhabited time and space as the episode demanded. He was without benefit of home, a continuous stranger, a visitor welcome or unwelcome each different time he disembarked. His roots were his steps along strange roads, his place was a ticket, and an eye pressed to a window to catch the fleeting face of new shores. Or of invented countries. Of romances broken off, that never were, perhaps. . . .

I lower the final page and stare out at the ceaseless barren acreage of the waves. My heart is overwhelmed with compassion, and a terrible awe, at my fellow-marooned's spiritual and literary achievement. Then another emotion begins to intrude. Pure and simple, it's envy. I curse, virulently, from the depths of my grudge-galled being.

And right then and there I undergo my epiphany. I blink at it. I swallow slowly, and I actually look around over my shoulder, before I throw back my head, and cackle deliriously up past my straw hat brim at the blank scalding heavens.

I will not — contrary to request — pass along this manuscript in a bottle. As is. I will commandeer it. These wave-borne memoirs, this sea-wrack testament, this multitudinous philosophical and poetic accounting, I will put forth as my own. Indeed I shall. Why not, it's a page right out of the original author's precepts! A mask to suit the narrative moment! As I forage for pen and buckled pad of paper stamped with the resort hotel's monogram, I burble in delight. I get to play my own heartless, monstrous practical joke, as payback for the one fate has pulled on me. In an unsteady hand I copy out a new version of the bottled preamble note, substituting info relevant to my airborne misadventure and ultimate location. I tear up the authentic, mold-blotched item. I insert my counterfeit into the plastic drinking bottle, and I cap it, and I heave it into the waves. I defy fate in its teeth with this puny, reckless gesture, even as I call upon my vessel the impossible luck of its inspiration.

The bottle bobs away. I pace up and down the scrawny fringe of beach in a disorder of exultation, my fingers crossed as I clutch to my breast the pages of my brand new self. I cackle, and wait to be published.

A week passes. Another week. A third. Nothing happens. And of course it never will, I begin to realize. Fate has just added one more taunt, one more ad hominem, to its trickery. I groan under my basket-cradle, and swat at the marsh bug buzzing at my ear. I slap, and then again, violently. I slap and pound to the point of savagery. But the bug is not at my ear.

I writhe to my feet and storm out to the rim of beach, flapping my arms and howling. The search plane swoops overhead, waggling its wings. Like a cartoon stork signaling an impending pickup. Down below I hop about, a bewhiskered, sinful newborn, beside himself at the prospect of his delivery, at the miracle of his treacherous, phony soul and story.

Conversation

CONVERSATION

May I sit?"

"Pardon?"

"I said, 'May I sit?' May I join you?"

"Not at all — I mean, of course, of course. No problem at all. Please —"

"I hope I'm not disturbing you."

"No, no. Just jotting a few notes in my journal, as you see."

"Indeed. That's why I decided to bring my coffee over here. You're a newcomer to our fair city?"

"Indeed I am."

"And what do you think of us?"

"Pardon me?"

"I mean how do you find us? Are you enjoying your visit?"

"Why yes, my goodness — marvelous. It's a wonderful city! And such pleasant folk. Such as yourself."

"You're too kind."

"No, no, I speak the truth. I've just now been thinking how —"

"Enough of this charade. Listen to me: I've got a gun."

"Pardon me?"

"I said: *'I've got a gun.'* "

"A — a gu —? I — look, is this some kind of joke?"

"Yes, of course. A joke! No gun at all, see?"

"But — what the — now look here, what's this all about? Why, this is an outrage!"

"Now, now, you must forgive me. I was just trying to be instructive. To keep you on your toes. So you'll be careful."

"Well, I'm very sorry, but how dare you go around —"

"It's my friend over there, you see."

"What *friend?*"

"Over there. It's him: he's the one. Not with a gun. With a big big knife."

"Oh it's a big knife he has, is it? Look here —"

"You understand now, I am not joking."

"And you understand, I'm calling the waiter right now, I've had enough of this. Waiter! Waiter!"

"Excuse me, but I am the waiter."

"No you're not!"

"Well, in the waiter's absence. Or should I say . . . 'indisposal' . . . there is only me. And yourself. And my friend."

"My god — What do you want? My money? My watch?"

"Of course, of course. And your shoes. And that fine new belt. And then there is the matter of your journal. . . ."

"*This?* But it's just notes, impressions — a traveller's banal personal observations and fancies! Not many observations either. Just fancies really — mostly that."

"Fancies, you say? Of what sort?"

"Why, just little — I don't know, whimsies. Imaginings. Really of no import!"

"May I?"

"Well — if you must. But they're of no value at all to anyone in the world but me, I assure you!"

(Reads) "Yes . . . I see what you mean. Go ahead, keep them."

NETTING

I doze in the twilight, listening to the ceiling fan clacking and thudding above through the mosquito netting. There's a knock at the door. I hear my name called. Slowly I rouse myself. It's the proprietor, in person, agitated. Someone is ill. "You must come, please," he insists. "Someone very sick, mister." I regard him in annoyance. I shrug. "Call a doctor," I tell him. I start to turn away. "Doctor, he coming, not now," the proprietor burbles. "Mister, you come right away please." I make a slack gesture of protest, and mutter something. But I don't have the will to shut the door on him.

His slippers flap ahead of me up the dim, oily-damp stairs. At the next floor he turns and beckons me to hurry. I mutter again and make a vague, mocking gesture back. I take my time. I see him standing like a pajama-clad sentry at a door partly ajar. Again I'm summoned to hurry. I reach the threshold and peer disapprovingly in, following the grandiose pointing of his hand. The shadowy room is much like the one I left downstairs: a rickety fan, a few clothes scattered over some once-substantial bags, a dim-shrouded occupied bed. I register a faint, offensive clamminess.

"Who is it?" a voice gasps from behind the mosquito netting. I swivel my head toward the proprietor. He looks back up at me. The question is repeated. "I — I'm told you aren't well," I announce, fumbling. I shuffle in an awkward step and glance over malevolently at my guide. But he's vanished. "Are you the doctor?" the voice calls out, laboring. I twist about helplessly, in consternation. "Is that the doctor!" the voice demands. "The doctor is on his way —" I stammer back. "He'll be here soon — I'm sure. Can I help you at all?" I offer lamely, grimacing at the odor that is now thick in the air.

"I don't need a doctor, I'm dying," the voice declares thickly. "I need —" Suddenly it gulps, and pants. "Come, sit over here, I need to tell you — some things —" it rasps. In multiple dismay, hesitating, I approach the shadowy bed, with its camouflaged, foul presence. I sit. The voice gives a strained laugh and proclaims its appreciation for my being like itself. "I couldn't have one of those —" it says, using an ugly term for the locals. I grunt in disapproval, and then in acute distress, listening to it begin to talk.

I sit in darkness now, by this ghostly, gross sepulcher in the making, and realize I'm taking a dying man's confession. I stare down at the obscured floor, shaking my head and squirming as the voice disgorges itself of the full dross of a lifetime's waste, its intimate, evil crimes, squalid losses. Wounds gnawing away unhealed at the bone of a man's conscience. The plaint drones on and on, the air seems to grow ranker. My heart trembles, and then clenches inside me. Shock and horror swarm over me. All at once I scream. I leap to my feet and tear the mosquito netting aside. A death's head figure gapes at me from the pillows. I grab it by the ears.

"That's my life story!" I scream, in panic. "Why are you confessing *my life story! My secrets* —" I wrench the hideous visage this way and that.

"Mister — mister!" a voice cries behind me, pulling at my shoulder. Suddenly I let go and lurch backward off balance into the dark room. I slump against a wall, rubbing the back of a quaking hand over my mouth. The fan clanks overhead. The proprietor leans in behind the mosquito netting and then turns back and stares at me.

The doctor and I sit in the hotel's dismal version of an outdoor cafe. A bloated moon sags in the frail thatches of the palm tree, like a sickened half-animate thing. "I'll make out the papers, they'll cart him off in the morning, and that will be the end of that," says the doctor. His dress and demeanor are well-bred but shabby, remnants of a training years ago in the home country. "You shouldn't overdo that in this climate," he adds, with a bland nod at the bottle from which I've just delivered myself another serving.

I stare somberly at my glass, keeping it on the table. The proprietor appears in the lamplight. His hands flutter and stab. "Tomorrow, you clear off, mister. You go," he says. "You hear me?" I flap my hand in reply. The doctor looks at me when we're alone again. "As a matter of fact, that's advice I would give you myself," he says. I don't answer. I've seen the ghost of myself. I stare swaying at the drink in my grip. I shudder. I raise my head, blinking. But he's not there. "Very good advice," he says, behind me now with his much-worn bag. "Listen to me, I know this country and its mysteries. It's no place for an uneasy soul. I make no judgments," he declares. "But just ask yourself: what would have happened if I hadn't eventually shown up?" He turns, and melts stiffly into the torpid darkness.

My Ship

MY SHIP

To distract myself, I build a model ship. It's a small passenger vessel, an old one with a single dirty funnel, bound for retirement in the home country after a final voyage from a faraway dusty southern colony. Through the seas it churns and labors, with a big hole in a forward ladies' room, which requires a pump racketing nonstop night and day. I try to construct the straining machinery of the pump, but my modeling skills aren't up to the level of detail. And besides, I don't really have all the time in the world.

I turn my attention instead to the minireplica of myself aboard. There I am years ago as a child, on the verge of a whole new universe, on my way from an outpost to great places I've dreamed and read and heard tell about.

I depict myself, appropriately, preparing for the shipboard festivities to mark the crossing of the equator. A children's costume contest is the feature (at least as I remember), there'll be judges and prizes.

My parents pitch in, and finally I'm ready: my father's baggy pants rolled up to my knees, his wide black shoes flopping on my feet, his big pin-dot tie around my thin young neck above his slack waistcoat. My schoolboy cap sits on my head; rouge shines in pink circles on my cheeks; thick dark lipstick distorts my mouth into a garish, doleful sag. For buckteeth, I have an orange rind inside out under my lips, cut jack-o'-lantern style.

So appropriately, so achingly to my grown mind now, this is how I cross my first equator — as a sad young homespun clown, wearing his parents' makeup and clothes. An award-winning clown, I'll note. I am voted First Prize in the judging, and receive a gift as resonant as my outfit . . . a bright painted tin globe of the world, with my name grandly engraved into a glossy midocean.

This is the icon of me on my ship. Not just a clown — an award-winning clown, with the shrunken hollow planet as his bauble! But this is not all that overcomes me, in the midst of my foolhardy bit of hobby for distraction. It dawns on me all at once who these figures really are, lending a hand to their son, there in the backstage of that slanting cabin on the laboring little ship with its gaping ladies' room.

My father there — that portly unshaven gent with his thinning hair flying up and his front false tooth out, wearing a food-stained shirt and, at midafternoon, pajama bottoms, with a frayed belt cinched over his potbelly to bolster the elastic waistband. My mother there beside him, in huge rimmed movie-star sunglasses, with a converted fruit basket upside down on her head, for a hat. The pompoms dangling from the brim are her extra touch of fashion transmutation.

In other words, a neophyte buffoon amateur — an innocent — being assisted onto the stage of life by two hardbitten, full-blown veteran buffoon professionals.

The insight is too piercing for me. I feel seasick. My rented tools — the awl and calipers, the tapping hammer, the carving blades — turn heavy and burdensome in my hands. I can't bring myself to finish constructing the models of my parents. I lose heart with the so-called amusement, which has turned into a creepy replica of my personal predicament as an adult. I pack the whole thing up in a box.

I do what I always do. I find a storage place in the neighborhood and lock away the dismal boat and its half-rendered occupants, and get a ticket for the lot. I throw this in with the disorder of my papers, onto the little heap of all the other tickets just like it.

PROBLEMS

I have passport problems, of a very particular kind. I sit in photographers' shops, straining and projecting, but the outcome is always the same. The photographer mops his brow and shakes his head. He stares again through the viewfinder and steps back in a quandary. He squeezes his eyes. He pulls and twists at the camera. But it's never any use. "Never seen anything like it!" he mutters. "Never!" The camera is switched for another. No matter. One of these picture-takers sums up my private nightmare in a simple phrase. "You poor, poor man . . ." he announces.

The passport camera points at me, and sees no one clearly. Just the shimmer of a visage. A face permanently out of focus. An unformed countenance that lacks the definitive human clarity of being a certain someone.

This is a shockingly intimate mirror of my private psychological state, and it has ominous consequences. How can I hope to negotiate the whole business of borders, of frontiers, of existential documentation? I try; but I become, at best, a laughingstock among the border personnel, with my requests, that in my case they match bearer to image by squinting at me. Or by having one or two drinks first. Or by allowing me to dash across their scrutiny in a blur.

I grow hugely unpopular with the orthodox masses of travellers in line behind me. Particular and specific faces snarl at me in multiple impatient languages.

On a couple of occasions, my odd requests result in being hauled away to jail, or getting the rough treatment ad hominem in a back office.

While other folk wing off to their exotic destinations on festive charter flights, I'm forced to bribe smugglers a small fortune just to steal an occasional holiday break. My travel modes consist of variants of suffocation: in the back of a van under an oil-stained tarp; down the queasy hold of a freighter; up in the chill rear storage of a small plane, flying without lights, piloted by thugs.

Finally I turn to counseling, thinking to engage my problem at its source. My personal history of rootlessness, of puerile self-absorption that trumpets, in obvious irony, a complete lack of self — all this is heard out with a few somber nods of a head. After a substantial silence, verging on the awkward, I'm presented with a long, slow sigh, and several minutes of expensive platitudes. Settling down, etc. I stop bothering to go.

Instead, mulling over my confessions, I bring out one afternoon my version of that private archive of snapshots we all carry with us as mementos of our grander journey, the one that began far away, at birth. With a pang in my heart I find here some clear images of this individual who I am. The items possess an odd frailty and pathos; they're from my early days. But my desperation inspires me to desperate ploys.

So a passport officer now scrutinizes in his rough grip the distinctive face of a schoolboy, shyly smiling on class day, in his cap and striped tie and blazer. Just beyond, in the flesh, a grown man laden with sporty luggage is grinning in a sickly, sweating way. Over and over again he proclaims, with a nervous solicitous laugh at the bizarreness of it all: "Yes, that's me, can you believe it? Peculiar, no? But that's me, honestly — in the most authentic, genuine sense, that's really me. That's me," he cries, glancing over his shoulder at the growling multitudes edging closer in their lines behind him.

PROTECTION

When I return from my walk to the ruins, there's a note slipped under my door at the little hotel. It's a warning, that an attack by pirates is imminent — and that every guest is expected to place his firearm at the service of the management.

I rush along the balcony and downstairs, in an uproar.

"What is all this about?" I demand, rattling the paper at the huffing woman who tends the desk. She's now wrenching a shutter closed. "You must bring your gun, right down here," she replies. "To protect us." "But why on earth would I have a gun!" I protest. "And protect against whom — what does this mean, 'pirates'?" I demand frantically. "Desperate men, *desperate men,*" she snaps back. "Is on the radio. Marauders. But how you not have no gun?" she cries, unwilling to believe my news. "You're a man, you say you're a traveller, yes? You must have means to defend yourself!" I shake my head, and fling up a hand at her insistence and ignorance.

"What I am is a *poetic* traveller," I inform her. "I take the chances of the road equipped with a journal," I explain, "to record my impressions. Plus a sketch pad and watercolors. But I'm really an indifferent artist," I confess. "I also carry a cheap camera, and a child's bouncing trifle I got at a street stall, to remind me of something dear years ago. That's what I have."

The woman stares at me and then claps her hands to her head.

"No gun!" she cries. "But how will we protect ourselves!" She starts wailing, and ponderously heaves herself about. "But surely someone else has a gun!" I protest. "No, no," she wails. "You the only guest, is the off-season." "But what about the hotel, it — my god," I squawk, "you can't expect your guests to supply an arsenal to defend the place!" But the woman isn't listening, she's fallen to her knees by the counter where she grimaces in fervent, terrified prayer.

I'm a quandary. I start back toward my room, but then I change my mind. With a thudding heart, I step outside, into the muggy temperate air. The beach and the inlet lie just thirty yards below. I scan them, and the empty horizon, and the small headland with its domestic crumble of ruins, from which I'd just returned. All is silent, with the sluggish stillness of late afternoon. But now this vista pulses with menace. I edge out a few feet more and peer frantically and absurdly left and right, looking for anything near the hammock, the scraggly picnic table, the beach chair, for use as a lethal weapon.

TERRA-COTTA

Under a grey obdurate sky, I locate the address I'm after. I walk up a brick path to a door and press the bell. The house is much the same as the rest of the side street, and as the whole town itself: well made, discreet, almost intentionally dowdy. The door opens. I swallow and mumble an explanation of who I am, to someone in an old-fashioned formally cut suit, and severe spectacles, through which he levels a polite impersonal gaze at me as he shows me into a front parlor. He goes through an inner door, leaving me seated amidst genteelly worn furniture and a dour opulence of Persian rugs. I glance at the soles of my boots nervously, for tracked dirt. I stare over hurriedly at the glass cabinets and their treasures.

The inner door opens, a second representative appears with the first. He greets me cordially. He is an older, balding version of the type, grey hair worn long and dressed back to the collar of his suit, which is even more outdated and formally cut than his associate's. His spectacles are pince-nez. He conveys the air of a long-established, unfrivolous and discreet authority and order — part banker, part butler.

He directs his associate to set on the low, dull-gilded table in front of me a shape draped in velvet. Underneath is my order. I shift onto the edge of my seat. The senior representative smiles ever so slightly. "Shall I?" he says, indicating the velvet. I nod. "Yes — please," I murmur. There's the soft gleam of cufflinks as he reaches down and deftly lifts. I blink. I peer in confusion.

"Is something unsatisfactory?" he says.

"But — I don't understand," I stammer, in dismay, confronted by the disorder of brownish clutter crowded onto flattened chunks of the world. "I asked for a commemorative miniature, based on my childhood home — a composite if necessary," I exclaim. "As a simple kind of talisman for good luck. As a lodestone to bear along with me, in my rootless adult wandering!"

"Indeed," he replies. "But I'm afraid we can only be faithful to the personal documentation that you've supplied us. Which was the hodgepodge of far-flung impermanences you see replicated before you," he declares.

"But this is just a jumble of sites and places, a cacophony!" I protest. "I wanted something as a psychological *anchor*, as an icon of *stability*. For all that money, couldn't you just have made something up, like one of those heartwarming traditional items over there in the cabinets?" I demand.

He stiffens. "Sir, we are a creditable firm of long-standing tradition!" he announces. The light glares on his pincenez. "Operating under the highest standards of service," he goes on. "We fashion quality poetic mementos of our client's early histories. We do not *lie*."

I flush. I stare back at the pathetic shambles and dislocations on the table in silence, my cheeks aflame with disappointment, with a complex shame that includes the stark shock of betrayal — at seeing what I hoped would be the last-ditch countercharm to the drift of my life, showing itself instead as a gigantic piece of incriminatory evidence.

"Now just a minute," I blurt out, pointing. "This is *clay*. You promised me lapis lazuli, or some such like!" "Sir, we guaranteed an appropriate precious material," he replies coolly. "That is our finest terra-cotta, whose exquisite fragility we thought perfectly reflected —" "All right, all right," I interrupt him. He sniffs and lifts his well-shaved chin. "Sir," he says.

Another long awkward silence in the carpeted, substantial room. I put my head in my hands and squeeze my eyes shut. "Sir, would you like it delivered somewhere?" his voice primly inquires. I look up at him slowly. "I'm staying . . . at the hotel, at the railroad station. . . ." I start to mumble back. But then it occurs to me I might want to move on again tonight. To somewhere else . . . not so very much different, really, from here.

The irony rings me like a bell caught in an unyielding grip.

"Never mind, I'll take it with me," I murmur. "We'll box it for you then," he says.

Back out in the street, the sky hangs lower, a wind rises. I have to somehow open my umbrella halfway back. I trudge along. The rain spatters loudly off the umbrella rim, onto the frail, cumbersome burden clinking under my arm at every step.

COMPANY

I get locked up in a foreign jail. "But what did I do?" I demand frantically. "Come on, you know why," I'm told. "No, I don't," I protest. "Please, what are the charges? What's my so-called crime or infraction?"

But the guard is already trudging away down the hall, tugging at his belt with its big keys jangling.

For a couple of weeks, I'm in a clamor of anguish. But then resignation sets in, nagged by a perpetual undercurrent of perplexity of course. But really what can I do, one lone drifting soul matched against fate in league with injustice?

My cell, it turns out, isn't altogether uncomfortable, albeit spartan and smelling of coarse disinfectant. But it's sunny, and through the window bars, if I twist my neck, I can see the pale green droops of a cactus plant and the distant shaggy heads of palms along the crumbling lane I was brought to get here. My food is tedious, conceived by someone obviously without culinary aspiration. But I'm nourished enough, and I have to say portions are adequate.

It's a small, obscure jail I'm in. I'm its lone prisoner.

I try to turn my incarceration to my advantage, to follow the grand tradition of my lot by undertaking a program of vigorous self-improvement. I meditate. I set myself to thinking positively in general, to keeping my spirits up, which is a serious undertaking, given the fading of days into weeks and then months, without a word of any kind about my case. Defiantly I strategize about how I'll really seize life by the horns and live it to its juicy marrow, once justice finally clutches its head in apology, and the day of my release dawns.

Each and every morning of captivity before that, I exercise. The guard, a fat harmless slouch of a fellow really, leans against the wall and watches, mouth open, as I go through my paces of jumping jacks and knee bends and push-ups galore. He rubs at the sweating back of his neck under its frayed, stained government-issue collar, and nods slowly, impressed.

I've given up on him long ago as a source of information. He's as ignorant as I am about the status of my case, of its undeclared charges and spurious so-called details. Perhaps there never were charges. Perhaps all this havoc in my life is owed to someone yawning and misfiling a piece of paper in an old city many miles and days away. My guard forever shrugs and scratches his neck. He only follows orders — of course, of course — and these come only once in a great while. Once a blue moon, in fact.

I think of this last phrase, and its forsaken implications, and I scramble down onto the floor of my cell again, and grunt away at push-ups until I'm stunned from lack of breath and my shoulders twang in outrage.

In these circumstances, one strange despair works its fingers into my heart. That, being in this isolation, I will lose all my finer social skills — the ones pertaining to the vibrant, thronging world out beyond my cell door, to which I'll be returned someday, doubtless, I pray.

So I set aside a strict hour daily, to practice sprightly

two-part conversations with myself, on various topics, large and small. But this is very cheap currency for the real thing. Eventually, I turn pleading to the guard. Out of a gruff kindness for my condition, or just as much a doltish indolence, he shrugs and goes along with me. So every evening, our forgotten little backwater jail presents a lantern-lit spectacle to the ponderous stars hovering in the semitropical night, to the crickets chaffing nonstop in the sagging cactuses.

"Hello there, friend!" I cry, through the rusty bars of my cell. "Hope I'm not scandalously late!"

A pause. "Go on," I mutter.

"No — you are — not —" recites the guard, as I've coached him. "My directions — to this charming — bistro — were complex —" he continues, laboring grimly at his lines. "I con — gratulate — you — on finding — it —"

"Thanks!" I cry, with animated bonhomie, nodding and giving thumbs-up to my partner's efforts. "Good company and good food are always inspirations to creative concentration!"

"Well said — friend!" rejoins the guard, and he grins wide in thespian pride. He tugs again at the done-up slovenly collar of his uniform and swipes at the dust of corn chaff from tending the scraggly pullet he keeps out behind the jailhouse. "Shall I —" he resumes. "Shall I — Shall —" A stricken pause. His face drops.

" 'Shall I summon the waiter,' " I murmur.

He nods and clenches his fists. "Shall I — summon — the waiter!" he barks.

And so forth we carry on, until the guard looks around his shoulder, panting, and takes out his big watch and announces, with a wrenching open of his collar button and a rolling of stubbly jowls in resumed authority, that time's up for the night.

I thank him. Somewhat reassured, I return to my perch on the coarse blanket of my bunk. The jail lantern is turned down. My erstwhile fellow bon vivant trudges out through the starlight to his small quarters in the rear, and I drift back to my gnawing prisoner's ruminations. I hear his noisy piss against the jail wall, and then his snores; and a bleak intimacy grips my heart in desperate comfort, until sleep shrouds everything away for its few grey forgetful hours.

Money

MONEY

I run out of money on the road, down south. Things get very bad. My pride, yet again, becomes soiled, debased. I fall in with a local who stands me a beer in the smoke and humidity of a run-down saloon. He hears my tale of adventuring life undone by finances, and he nods, blinking narrow, reddened eyes under his crumpled porkpie fisherman's hat. He rubs a bulky knuckle along his cheek stubble. I stare despondently at the level in my bottle. He suggests another round, and I accede, apologetically, grateful and made childish, shamed. He claps me on the back and pronounces a cliché about hard times, etc. He looks at me.

He leans in and murmurs that he knows how I could earn some quick money, if I cared to. I blink back at him. I don't find him much to my liking, despite his hospitality. He has a nasty smell about him, like worms for bait. "What's that?" I ask guardedly. He grins. He peers around over a shoulder and leans in again and whispers. I stiffen, as if a snake had slid against my foot. I turn toward him, aghast. "But that's —" I tell him, pronouncing the nightmarish words. He shrugs. He wears a cool, patronizing smile on his slabby face. "Call it whatever," he says. "It ain't nice and clean, but it pays for drinks, I'll tell ya that. And a room, and a bus ticket," he adds. He salutes with his beer and tilts it to his mouth, and nods for me to help myself to mine. He watches me sidelong under his hat. I remain stock-still for a moment, there in the dingy smoky dimness. Then I twist my head away, from him and his words. I stare off at the grime of the floor, shaking my head in open distress, in protesting revulsion at who I've fallen among, owing to lack of means.

The job comes two nights later. We bump along the dirt road in his truck, lights off. I drink from the common half-pint of rye to deaden my nerves and my conscience, my chattering teeth. He has a bottle of beer open between his legs. The foul odor like bait invests the cab around us.

Eventually we see the telltale white picket fencing. We pull over in stealth under an oak tree, Spanish moss clanking on our roof. The site is extensive, being the main resting place for this corner of the county. We get the shovels and the crowbar from the back. Scanning to make sure the watchman's lantern is nowhere about, we scramble over furtively to the gate, where he pries the lock, and we slip in.

The moon is big, but discolored, and goes in and out of clouds. We hurry along after the beam of his flashlight, into the first rows of headstones and statuary, among the willows and stark tomb masses. I'm quaking. I feel surrounded not by death, which seems abstract and clean, but by deadness, which is grossly corporeal, inert, ghastly. We have trouble locating the proper grave, from the directions of the cousin of his, who works at a funeral home. He curses as we backtrack. I bite my lip.

Finally he stops us at a freshly dug plot, in a new crowded section. We start in with the shovels. Our arrangement is I will work until we've bared the coffin. Then I will stand watch while he does the gruesome business of extracting the valuables. After the first couple of shovelfuls, a recollection that I've been keeping at bay overwhelms me — my last time at a grave with spade and earth. A family sacrament. I groan and throw down the shovel and turn away, clutching at my ears at what I've sunk to. "What is it?" he cries, in a whisper. "What's the matter?" I shake my head, gnawing at my wrist. "Listen," he hisses. "Whatever it is, you pick up that damn shovel, and you get back at it, or they'll find us like a couple of chickens standing in the pot when they come open up in the morning! You hear me?" he threatens. I twist my head from side to side, in turmoil. Then I nod. I grit my teeth. I wipe my sleeve over my face and get back to work, trembling. Desperately we root away.

My shovel clinks. I heave it aside, as if it were alive with worms. I scramble backward up the slope of fresh earth we've made. The local stares up at me, his heavy face oily with sweat under the clownish fisherman's hat. He reaches over for the crowbar. "I'll go keep a lookout," I tell him. "You see a light, you come right back here on the run," he instructs. "And *quiet*." He bends and starts to feel along the coffin lid for a prying point.

I duck my head from the sight and stumble off. I sway down a grassy row of lugubrious statuary. I wrench the bottle from my back pocket and guzzle a long, harsh swallow. I pause, panting, and smear at the sweat dripping off my nose. My blistered hand stings. I drift hesitantly on. The dim graveyard spreads away around me, implacably somber, desolate, utterly still but for the thin clinking and transgressive squeaking off somewhere behind me. I shudder. I am at a junction of funereal rows, a sepulchral crossroads. The moonlight all at once floods full for a moment, and then dissolves away, like a great lamp switched on then off in a deserted silent house. I stare wide-eyed into the black threshold of a tomb across from me. A mist flickers.

My throat closes. My nerves flare into every shrill pore of me. Tears well from my eyes. I jibber in terror, as two misty forms sway under the lintel of the tomb entrance. Tortured, elongated elderly faces take shape.

"Shame on you . . . for what you've come to. . . ." an intimate old-woman's voice laboriously warbles.

My hair stands on end. I barely hear the words in the stun of my pulse. "M-m —" I bleat, my jaw locked.

"Shame . . . on . . . you. . . ." a second wobbly, chambered voice echoes.

In slow motion, I lurch backward and flounder off down the row I'd come. I swarm along as if through swamp mud, jelly legged, gurgling half words. I heave around a cluttered corner. Ahead shows the outraged grave, then the upper part of the local, under his hat, as he straightens from his work to look around. I catch sight of the forced coffin lid by him and I swerve down onto my knees in the grass, as if from a blow. I burble, flapping my hands.

"Christ, will you keep quiet!" he snarls, climbing up toward me. "What in hell's name — is it ghosts?" he demands. I nod, stark eyed. "My p-p-parents —" I get out, in agony. "Th-they s-s-saw me." I claw at my mouth. "Will you shut up!" he hisses. "That watchman carries a pistol, you hear me? You want to find out how good a shot he is?" He stares off from where I'd come. "I know them two, they're a menace," he mutters. "They ain't your goddam parents." He bends back to the grave soil and gets a shovel. I watch him head off. "What are you going to do?" I cry. "To get rid of them!" he mutters over his shoulder. "Stay here." "Wait!" I protest. I trail him in hectic confusion.

He stalks along until he reaches the junction of the rows. I hang back, gesturing in uncertain protest, as he edges forward sideways toward the tomb, in his battered hat, hefting the shovel. He calls out in a suppressed voice. My heart swells in my throat. I jerk a hand. The ghostly shapes sway up in the tomb mouth. I gasp, and shrink back. There's a low quarreling of voices. The local prods and menaces with the shovel, wields it like a club. The shapes flicker in agitation, they writhe and twist about; then they fizzle away, into the blackness of the tomb.

Their vanquisher waits to make sure they're gone. He turns and trudges back toward me. "Now enough of that, and quit carrying on like a little girl!" he pants. "You hear me?" I nod, staring down to the side, too shamed and overcome to lift my head. As he moves on by me, the breeze stirs the odor of bait from him, freshly intense, ghastly. I notice all at once the soiled dampness of his robbing hands. I stiffen in dawning horror. I wrench away. He plods out of sight around some dark winged silhouettes. I lurch over to a headstone and sink down behind it, hanging on as I'm sick to my stomach.

I make my way back feebly, hearing his impatiently whispered calls. I help him fill in the grave. Finally we tramp back toward the gate with the shovels. He rises ponderously on tiptoe every now and then, glancing left and right. He smirks at me, rank with sweat. "Your *p-p-parents* . . ." he repeats, and shakes his head. "Not your line of work, I guess," he mutters. I stare dully down at the grass, holding my breath at his odor, ashen faced, my jaw clenched. The shovel feels made of lead on my shoulder. He sighs, and hefts something once again in his dirty hand, something old and precious and infinitely private. It glints for a moment in the dim moonlight. He winks under his hat. "Well you tell your parents, whenever you see 'em, your share of this came in real handy," he declares. "For all those travels you like to go on about," he says.

CAMPFIRE

I make my campfire by the side of the road. Sad grey folk drift out from the cold woods and settle by the rim of the flames. They're the ghosts of travellers, like myself, who've gone before me. I poke at the fire and hunch stolidly in my coat, and they start up their round of tales. Ghosts telling stories in the firelight. They groan and murmur at what haunts them: memory, regret. The night wind rummages with its stony fingers in the burning embers and knotted brush. I nod, my eyes welling, as one in rags laments a love abandoned in a strange country, out of selfishness and pride, out of a traveller's false extravagance of self-regard. Regretted ever since . . . like an early death. The speaker's quavering face is gaunt from remorse, from the torments of memory.

I keep my peace, full of my own thoughts, waiting for the flames to ebb away and break up this company. But why am I among them, they want to know. One like me, still in the midst of his days. Or rather, here on the broken margin. They chide me in their dreary way on the vainness of the traveller's life. On the desolations of the cold woods. But I just settle further in my coat, stolidly waiting them out, staring into the dying flames.

THE PALACE

I arrive at a court, after a long journey. It's a place from a fairy tale — high alabaster turrets, a courtyard garden with fruit trees in perpetual bloom, with peacocks wandering about, nodding and stately, and swans clambering in through the main gate shaking the water of the moat from their wings.

I am given a lovely chamber, with a maiden to attend me and a songbird in a cage on my balcony. I soak away the dirt of months of travel in a marble tub. Then my attendant helps me into silken robes, and I'm no more the haggard, numbed wanderer brought along here in the morning. I'm a man of the world again, who has seen far places, and has stories to tell.

At the long, opulent table, I regale the royal company with episodes from my journeys, with illuminations and astounding vistas: a snowstorm rescue in a landscape of glass mountains; a herd of animals leaping backward in lumbering flight through the wastes of antipodal deserts. The lake where a town floats on an island made of reeds and flowers, and at night the native women wear candles in their hair.

I expound on the ways of these candlelit women for the sake of the princess of the court, who listens spellbound, cross-legged on her pillow with her golden, laden fork suspended in midmotion. "The one judged loveliest of these womenfolk, Your Highness," I address her, "earns the right to wear a prize mantle, constructed entirely from drugged fireflies."

I mime delicately the form of the mantle, and the young princess touches a hand to her head, in duplication, and blinks her green eyes at me.

Artfully I turn to a different part of the table, and compliment my royal host on the glories of his palace, compared to which all others are but a gathering of reeds in the water. I raise my glass in a guest's dexterous toast, and gracefully acknowledge the expressions of approval around me.

After retiring, I doze among embroidered pillows, listening to the songbird, contemplating shadows, thinking of green eyes. A voice whispers in the darkness — my attendant. Rising on my elbow I scan by candlelight the note she's brought. My heart hurries.

I slip out from my chamber and follow her down a back stairway. She halts, and gestures with discreet, urgent grace. A veiled figure awaits me in the shadows of a corner of the garden. Green eyes gaze up at me over the alluring modesty of draped chiffon.

The princess and I stroll under the sculpted globes of the trees studded with their pale, scented fruits. High over the turrets the much-travelled moon hangs, like an old, burnished ornament. The princess has me talk again of my travels, of the reed island in particular, and its women, and their practices. Then we fall silent, and we drift to a halt, to the sound of our heartbeats. The moon catches her gauzy veil so it seems to glow. Her green eyes are dewy. She murmurs under her chiffon. "Hero . . ." is all I can hear. My heart flutters in my breast. I raise a hand that trembles to the side of her face, and lift away the veil, and uncover the

loveliness of her royal, youthful face. I bend close, and our
lips meet, soft and long, in the moonlight of the palace,
among the turrets and fruit trees.

A tear rolls down the stubble of my cheek. I brush it
away with the grimy knuckle of a thumb, and stare, blinking and heart-pierced, into the mist of remembrance. A
voice breaks in on me. The boy is back with the donkey and
my meager, squalid load of bags. He gestures down from
where we've come and on ahead, at the dusty, relentless distances of the road. I blink at him, and flap my hand at his
bawling insistence. I mutter an ill-tempered phrase.
Phlegmatically I rise, one knee at a time. I gaze a long time
back the way we've come in haste. Then I turn and I follow
after him, to resume my wanderings, until the next brief
transformation at another gilded distant court, with its
floating of tales ... its brief, furtive, heart-wrenching
memories.

The Porter's
Joke

THE PORTER'S JOKE

After much difficulty, I hire the closest thing to a passable helper from the dingy lot assembled in the dawn mud of the courtyard. Together we set out into the interior.

We slouch along by mule through humid uplands. Very soon it becomes clear my porter is as odd as the scraggly, jerry-rigged turban on his head. What I took for a faint light of native intelligence in his brown eyes is actually the glint of a loose screw. He chatters away at me nonstop in tribal pidgin; he reins to a halt just to deliver a burst of song. He yelps and charges off the path like a schoolkid under the flocks of iridescent honey birds, which erupt wheeling overhead into the early twilight from the dark canopies of the trees. My sharp cries finally bring him back.

I try my best to ignore him. He makes our meager campfire with great fanfare, and serves up the powdered stew with a lavish rolling of eyeballs at such splendor. I tip my hat brim slowly back on my head. I prod my spoon about in the tin plate, and wonder how I'm going to put up with him for the days ahead, on such an intimate mission.

In the middle of the night, he goes a step further. A short scream, like a bark, jolts me awake. I hear struggling from close by — his tent. I shout and snatch up my big flashlight and revolver and rush out into the dark, plowing in my untied boots. With a hammering heart I throw open the flap of his tent. He gapes at me wildly, naked headed in the shaft of my light. His sleeping carpet is tangled about him. There's a frozen, stricken moment. Then he throws back his head, and roars and points at me. "Joke," he cries. He nods over and over. "Joke!" I blink in amazement. "You — idiot," I snarl. I curse him and deliver a jumble-booted kick at his carpet. He yelps. He cowers away, looking crestfallen, sticking out his bottom lip like a surprised, hurt child. Above us, the tree rodents screech and thrash in the nocturnal branches.

Back in my tent I lie in the darkness seething, muttering to myself in fury at this intrusive, crackpot burden on such a delicate, and intimate, enterprise.

The next morning he's all obsequious good behavior. He grins at me with rotten teeth and bobs his turbaned head and hops about fixing coffee and packing the tents. A couple of times he claps his hand over his opening mouth, in a big show of self-restraint at the impulse of a song. I eye him sourly from my maps.

We head off. What I'm after should be a day or two's ride farther in. My porter minds himself and keeps quiet. But by midday he can't help it, a few cautious scraps of chatter and song get loose. He winks at me, to excuse them. By late afternoon he's back to babbling nonstop and flailing his arms at all the traffic in the trees around us.

We come out into a broad, open acreage, carpeted with giant flat-blossomed crimson poppies, like an epic festive plaza of crepe-paper cobblestones. We walk our mules, which are laboring after hard going. "This sort of terrain is prime for snakes," I warn. My helper goes barefoot. I tell him to put on his boots. He shrugs. I repeat my instruction,

twice, before finally he yanks his mule to a stop. He makes
a display of rummaging about in his saddlebag. He brings
out crumpled boots and starts laboriously to pull them on,
pouting up at me like a disgruntled ten-year-old.

All at once he screeches. He grabs at a lower leg and hops
on one foot, and then collapses, squawking in pain. He
points a jabbing finger at the crimson blossoms nearby. "My
god — a snake — where is it?" I shout. I flounder by the
side of my mule, grabbing at the revolver on my jodhpured
hip. Both our animals bellow and rear. The porter goes suddenly rigid. He gapes at me. Then he roars like he did last
night. He throws his head from side to side, grabbing his
stomach in mirth. "Joke!" he cries, gesturing at my foolishness. "Joke! Joke!"

I barely hesitate. I stalk over to him and clap my right
hand to my left shoulder. I backhand him full-force, catching him violently on the side of his thin-whiskered cheek.
His turban shoots off into the air. He sprawls into the poppies. "Are you mad?" I demand, standing over him, chest
heaving. "If you ever do that again — I'll shoot you, do you
hear me? I'm not going to have my intensely private business disrupted by your crazy mischief!" I snarl. I have my
hand tight around my revolver. He stares back at me from
the crimson blossoms, a hand at his cheek. His eyes are wide.
Then for just a moment, an astounding infantile rage
flashes in them. His hand gropes behind the back of his
soiled robe. Then the heat in his eyes fades, turns flat, sulky.
He bobs his head and grins in mawkish, petulant shock. But
his eyes don't lose their hooded malice.

I watch him crawl over to the turban and climb to his
feet, resetting his headgear, fumbling. He grins and nods
away at me, holding up a trembling hand to proclaim the

full scope of his chastisement. In silence I have him mount up and take the lead, so I can keep him in my sights.

We continue on through the red acres. The dark wall of the forest looms up in the distance. Every so often he turns around on his mule, to bob and grin back grotesquely at me in ongoing acknowledgment of his transgressions. But his eyes play a different game. Around us, the afternoon light slowly begins to wane. We will have to make camp in a while. I turn over in my mind what the evening will bring; and grimly, what I see for tomorrow.

I see our afternoon arrival at the pool marked by the three jagged rocks, like a mammoth's mossy teeth. Behind them drops a steep gully. There somewhere, deep in the clay, lie what all these efforts are after: a certain memento, valuable to no one but me, which time's vandals years ago looted and vengefully hid away here. Buried under a great boulder that will take two men to dislodge, which is why I need a helper.

I see the dappled sunlight around us as we finally stand gazing down into the gully, me and my insufferable porter. I send him scrambling down first, and I follow, sliding. I wrench my ankle when I land. He regards this with a slight, alert angling of his turbaned head. I grit my teeth against the pain and hobble over to the boulder, where I've ordered him. We set ourselves, and strain; we strain, and the boulder moves. It moves again. Panting, I have him begin with the shovel. I harangue him on, staring into the clay for the first glint of painted tin. He grunts and tips out the slow shovelfuls behind him. Suddenly I shout and wave him clear. I clamber down, wincing, and start gouging away barehanded. The porter squats on his heels a few yards off, looking on, the sweat dripping from under his askew tur-

ban. With a cry I hold up in trembling grimy hands a little
arc fragment of tin bauble. Emotion swells through me and
I blink away tears.

Suddenly I spin around. He's moved, I realize. Just a foot
or so over. He grins at me, still streaked with sweat. His eyes
are very narrow. He cradles one arm peculiarly against his
waist. I see the grimy wrist. "What have you got there?" I
demand. "You dug up something! Give it to me!" I shout,
my voice cracking. I thrust a dirty hand at him. He grins
back, with awful teeth. He shakes his head. A reckless flame
dances openly in his eyes. "Give it to me — no joke!" I
scream. He doesn't reply. His other hand wanders behind
his back.

I fumble my revolver out and point it at him at arm's
length. His hand stops, out of sight. He stares down at me
with glittering eyes, grinning.

"Give it back, it means nothing to you," I murmur,
through clenched teeth. I sound almost desperate, my wavering gun in one hand, grubby trinket part in the other.
The stillness of deep afternoon lies all about us, like the heat
of an empty school yard around a tableau of bewitched tru-
ants.

I cock back the hammer of the revolver. "All right, you
want a joke, how's this?" I softly announce, tears of outrage
welling and the pain throbbing from my ankle. "How about
I just pull the trigger, and be done with all your malevolent,
infantile complications, for good? How about it?

"How about it?" I ask him. . . .

This is the scene, and the question, that passes in detail
before my mind, as the first touches of twilight fall across
us on our mules, and we leave the field of poppies and enter
the dimness of the trees.

FALLEN TREE

A huge tree falls, blocking the roadway with its massive barricade of branches and leaves. The coach driver shouts. Horses snorting and leering, the carriage shudders to a halt. It lumbers to turn itself about in the road, and makes its way back to the inn. I huddle in the depths of my seat, throbbing with despair.

"Don't worry," declares the innkeeper, jovial in his green hat with its upright feather. "We're old hands at these little catastrophes, these delays to a journey." He sighs wittily. "Now you're stranded — can't go anywhere for a while. Just here with us!" He leans in, elaborating his pleasantry. "You can't bear to part from us, we know!" he says. He winks, and laughs. He rubs his hands. "Wait till you see what we'll do with all that wood out there," he exclaims. "What a boon for us, and our craftsmen!" He snaps his fingers for a costumed helper, who takes my carefully packed bag and leads me up in his noisy boots and decorated suspenders to the room I'd left only hours ago at dawn.

The door shuts, and the full weight of insupportable calamity sinks over me. The tree in the road crushes away my courage, like a catastrophic blow to all possibilities. Like a stark final verdict, here among the high sunny valleys and shadowy hillsides. In strange agitation, I dig a small pistol from my bag with its cache of out-of-date guidebooks and puny fetishes, and pull the needleworked coverlet over my head on the bed, and prod the trembling gun to my temple. I moan once. The blast is abrupt and muffled. Reddened bits of goosedown spray into the air and drift back down around me like strange snow.

The rest of the morning, and all afternoon long, the inn folk bustle and swarm over the fallen greenery in the road. Saws and axes labor with exuberance. An accordion plays at the lunch break, there's singing, a group of fellows in suspenders show off their muscles and blisters to the serving girls. At twilight, big sledges piled high with great trimmed boughs and lengths of tree trunk come dragging along toward the inn, behind the plodding work ponies. A young drover perches on top of each, waving his cap in the blue and yellow dusk.

The innkeeper looks on, smiling in approval. Glass of new wine in hand, he goes out to greet the sledges, to select the very best of this boon for the inn's craftshop. The old woodcarvers stand by in their aromatic workroom, ready to fashion from obstruction the region's famous bounty of knickknacks and cuckoo clocks, like the one ticking down the hallway — *tick-tock* ... *tick-tock* — from the darkening, still room where I lie.

Clouds

CLOUDS:
A PICNIC STORY

1.

A couple of soldiers find me wandering in a daze, and bring me under guard to their stronghold. They wear bird's-nest helmets. I myself make quite a picture of harrowed travel: I'm in my signature costume of these days, which is by now threadbare plaid pajamas, and slippers. I'm temporarily blinded, too, from the closer brilliance of the sun in these parts. I must appear like a sleepwalker who has rambled out into the middle of his dreams.

Which is in fact what I am.

When my vision recovers, I find the stronghold sits on a long, formidable cloud high in the northern sky. It's a bulwark of an older barbaric style, with palings and ramparts of rough-split wood, and lots of massive stone and icy cloudmud. Indoors, things are primitive, but commodious. Heaps of the local version of treasure lie piled about in almost childlike disorder. Childlike too is the mix of valuables: ribbon bits, clumps of pollen, glittery metal filings from shop floors, all blown aloft by the relentless scraping wind from the world below . . . and now heaped beside clods of mineral still in their dirt, such as green jasper, and rare yellow quartz, almost flawless, hacked out from brief forays down onto peak tops. I note all this, recognizing my fondness for the ways of children's adventure tales.

I make my debut, blinking, at the court of the chief who presides over this rough, airy principality. A meal is served in smoky glass bowls. The chief is a ponderous sort, with a long lumpish egg-shaped face, and squinty eyes under the other egg shape of his turban of dyed cobwebs. In his garish brocaded robe he bids me give an account of myself. I do so, clad in my pajamas, my road-torn slippers.

"I'm a dreamer," I declare, quietly and wearily. "One lost in the perpetual realm of his dreams, hoping against hope to awaken. . . ."

The chief's daughter stares at me with innocent fascination. She is slightly cross-eyed, but also young and lively and winsome, in a way all so familiar to me. A snowy feather nods from the tip of her cobweb turban. "You must tell us what you dream," she cries, "right this minute!" She has a peremptory air, like a child's, and is addressed by her father tenderly as "Your Highness," as if she were a princess.

I shrug, and sigh, knowing what's to come. I do as bidden, as a guest has to.

"I dream I'm high up in the clouds," I recount. "In a curious fortress where the chief is a grand fellow in a turban and robes of brocade, and his royal daughter —"

The chief interrupts, scandalized. "But that's us!" he cries over his spoonful of bird's meat and miniature potatoes. He lowers the spoon into his bowl with a splash. "But that means we're all just — figments — in your dream!" he puffs.

I shrug once more, on a note of courteous and ineffectual resignation.

"Oh, but Father, how exciting!" the chief's daughter protests. Her cheeks are glowing. "I've always wanted to be in someone else's dream!"

"No, no, this is intolerable," the chief huffs. His eyes blink away feverishly. "What about all my costly minerals — my green jasper and rare yellow quartz, almost without flaw? What about my colorful bits of ribbons? Are they all just figments?"

The chief bubbles in great dark consternation, and my debut dinner is ominously broken off.

The daughter calls on me afterward with her chaperon. I step out from the uneasy moonlight of my chamber onto the coarse flagging of the hall. "You must not pay attention to Father, he loves his moods," she instructs me, with a shy pretense of imperious gaiety. Then she glances at the chaperon, and commands to hear the origins of my extraordinary condition. I grunt in melancholy. I gaze out beyond her at the starry sky through a crudely made arch.

I repeat yet again my account of having dozed off in the midst of my writing workday. As simple as that. . . . And how angry — how angry — my girlfriend — would be . . . were she to find me so. There in that banal, lost room . . . a world away. . . . I give a little laugh, wan and self-deprecating, at the trivial cause of all that has followed.

"Oh, you have a girlfriend," the daughter of the cloud chief exclaims, trying not to look a bit crestfallen and put out.

I have to smile privately, and poignantly, at the both of us. "Yes, and I love her very much," I reply, serving the fiction. "Shall I describe her to you?"

"Yes, you must, you must," the chief's daughter murmurs.

I do as bidden.

"But then she looks just like me!" the daughter exclaims, slyly, wide-eyed, when I'm done. I nod, with a private smile again. The daughter throws a quick beam of glee at her chaperon. "You must stay, so you can tell us all about your dream adventures!" she announces. "And I shall talk to Father, he must forget all about his silly minerals and riches! Yes, he must," she insists.

Her diplomacy seems to hold the following day. I accompany the eccentric court as it goes hunting in the air. For the enterprise the chief dons a brocaded bubble-shaped cap with immense round earflaps, and a quilted cloth breastplate of many strange colors. He is curt and brusque with me, but his wrath seems to have ebbed.

The hunt proceeds as follows: the chief and his retinue struggle onto a cloud that's dark and heavy with rain, and ride it like a barge as it sinks toward the lower terrain of the stratosphere, where game is within reach. There is much clamor and pomp and flying of pennants in all this. Once the hunting grounds are attained, a great net of the most gossamer filament is thrown blossoming wide into the air, then trolled through the wind for prey. Falcons and hawks swoop up and are entangled, as is a hardy little high-flying bat, all snow white in its fur. At one point the net traps a buzzard by mistake, and then the whole barge-cloud teeters and goes into an uproar as it's dragged along by this mammoth flailing brute of the air — until the net is abandoned, and the buzzard goes thrashing and tumbling into the distance. Finally the expert of nets is helped to his special perch, to fling the most exquisite, barely visible silken web imaginable. Lightning flickers in the cloud bottom. The netman casts, and then hauls in his catch of metal dust, and scraps of burst balloons, and shorn butterfly wings carried aloft in the whirling unceasing wind.

The chief's daughter and I observe the course of the day

while we pace a fair-weather cloud just above. Isn't it true that people can fly in their dreams, and have I? she wants to know. I answer to both in the affirmative, shading my eyes still from the glare. The daughter swallows, entranced. She wears a bubble cap of her own, with tassels at the flaps. And have I ever had adventures underwater for hours and hours, and been changed into another thing? I laugh, out of stirred affection. "I can tell you about my dream in an oasis with a sorcerer monkey," I tell her. "And a voyage I took through poppies and mountains, for the sake of a trinket." "For a trinket . . ." she repeats. "And what do you dream," she wonders, "in the nights of your dreams?" I have to grin at this, and make a gesture. "That's really quite a question," I inform her. "But I want to hear more about your girlfriend!" she demands. "Of course . . ." I reply, growing abstracted. A long sigh escapes me, and I scan about where I am, lost in the clouds of my own dreaming. "Yes, I've arranged it all with Father," the chief's daughter goes on gaily, "and it's all settled. You will stay with us and be my tutor, and every day you'll tell me another dream, and we will discuss it. Only you must be polite," she declares, "and not speak of your dreams in front of Father." I nod, gratefully, and quite sincerely so. My gaze lingers on her cross-eyes, her soft cheeks, until I catch myself and glance over at the chaperon, and nod again, with decorum. The chief's daughter claps in delight. "Here they come, oh look how much they've caught!" she cries.

The hunting party has transferred to a lighter cloud, and now they sail up toward us with their bounty, pennants flapping in the early twilight in satisfied pageantry.

Late that evening, I sit brooding on my thoughts in the lamplight of my chamber. There's a soft, unexpected knock on my door. I turn my head. Vanity and pleasure mix with a note of concern at this rapidity of the inevitable. I rise and cross to the door. "Your Highness?" I murmur, half-reproving, half-tweaking intimately. I open up a discreet amount and then the door is slammed in on me with rude violence.

The daughter's diplomacy has failed, I realize.

Two barbarous thugs in bird's-nest helmets swarm on top of me. One claps a hand over my mouth, to silence my protests, as the both of them drag me struggling out into the hall, and then beyond. I feel the night wind, suddenly, I see the stars wheeling above me. They force back my head, our struggles silhouette against starlight. A wedge of smoky glass flashes above me. My blood jets. My headless carcass is flung over the side of the cloudy wooden parapet, to tumble out into the dark sky.

A while later, there's a sharp knock on the door of the chief's daughter as she sits at her dressing table before bed. The chief enters, unbidden, carrying a dripping basket. He wears his long pompommed sleeping cap, but also still his quilted hunting vest. His cheeks are oddly flushed.

"Here," he squawks, in the awfulness of his authority. "Here is your dreamer — and he'll have little of his insolent dreams to recount anymore!"

He snatches the lid from the basket and displays its open maw. His daughter screams and leaps to her feet, her hands at her mouth. "And I hope this serves you as a lesson," the chief continues, squawking, but unsurely now, taken aback by his daughter's response. She shrinks away from him, and then all at once leaps forward and grabs the basket from his grip.

"Get out, get out!" she shouts. She batters her father, who retreats a step at a time, in utter confusion at her ferocity, until he is out of the room. She slams the door and turns the big key.

She comes back with the basket and sets it on the table. For a moment she recoils in fresh horror. Then she reaches in and, moaning with shock, she lifts out my head and places it by her mirror. She finds a scarf to sop the blood, and fits the blue-knotted ribbon for the door key over my brow, as a garland. With trembling, bloodied fingers she arranges the key by my ear. "There now, there now," she murmurs, and she sinks back quaking into her chair. "Now I have you to tell me all your dreams, whenever I wish," she declares, and she touches a trembling hand to her own head. "And first — first you must tell me a dream that's all about me," she goes on erratically, her voice laboring and thinning. "Yes, you must. . . ."

On the dressing table, my head tilts at an undignified angle, from the raggedness of the assault and the various personal items I'm propped on. A melancholy, astounded smile flickers over my ashen lips. My eyes are closed, shadowed. I try to accommodate her in my feeble voice, with a frail giggle of trauma at the monstrous impossibility of it all. I begin to recount the events of the last day or so, here in the clouds, bit by bit as they've transpired. The chief's daughter listens fixedly, over the pounding at her door, the cries.

Far below my headless body slowly plummets, wheeling down through the bastions of night, in bloody pajamas, in slippers, toward the dark ground.

2.

A woman laughs, peering down at me. She wears a golden mask across her eyes. Green feathers trail out from it.

"I've been delegated to come and fetch you," she declares merrily. "Because we all agree: it's not fair for the best costume of the night to spend his whole time lounging alone out here on the terrace! Are you too snobby for us?" she demands. "Or are you shy?"

She laughs again. She has a fruity English voice. She vibrates a rococo fan. The lamplight from French doors behind her gleams on the satin wealth of her gown.

I gaze at her, blank, stupefied. My hand fumbles suddenly where my face should be. I gasp out of dazed shock.

The woman laughs yet again, with a flutter of awkwardness.

"A man of mystery," she chides. "Well, you have too many admirers inside who won't be ignored!" she announces gamely. "So come along now —"

She reaches down to me where I'm sprawled on my back behind a marble bench, and grips my pajamaed sleeve.

"Wait . . . just a minute," I mumble, in turmoil and disbelief. She labors to get me to my feet. Finally I sway off-balance, vaguely upright. The woman steers and shoves me forward, tottering toward the latticed blaze of the French windows. She laughs, panting a bit, at my uncertainty of foot.

"Here he is, everyone!" she cries as we come inside. "Our headless wonder himself!"

Shouts of approval and clapping greet her announcement. I tilt from side to side, dazzled. About me glows what appears to be a living room, of an upper-class country house of an English-weekend type. There seems to be a costume party in progress: masked women in elaborate masquerades lounge and chatter among the furnishings; masked men hover brightly over them in fancy dress. The air is lively, chic, smokily festive in a bygone way. "I've brought him in to explain his secret to us!" my retriever proclaims. With a flourish of her fan, she steps back away from me.

"Speech, speech," shouts a tall man in a vast stark ruffle at the mantelpiece.

I stir a hand inarticulately, at a loss still from the shock of events.

"Oh, do tell!" a woman's voice pleads.

"Cat got your tongue?" a wag throws in, to a burst of quick laughter. "Lost your head?"

"He needs a drink!" cries someone.

A glass is thrust into my grip. I manage a little salute with it, to the crowd of expectant, smiling faces.

I hear my voice issuing somehow, from somewhere, faint and fugitive.

"You see — I'm having — a dream," it trembles, "and I can't — seem —"

"Speak up," someone interrupts.

"Looks more like a *nightmare* to me!" another quips, to a swell of mirth.

"Yes, considering — you're — in it," I hear myself rejoin softly, to an outburst of delighted approval.

The object of my riposte, a thick young gent in harlequin tights, grins in good sportsmanship. Unbelievably, I realize, my narcissism has been stirred by the presence of an audience. I sense myself actually assembling a soft, debilitated verve, like a very sick patient gracefully enduring the presence of bumptious visitors.

"But how d'you do it?" cries a voice. "How's it look so real?"

"All in the — imagination," I reply, dazedly warming to my repartee . . . to the occasion in general.

My tone now is quaking and fatigued, but somehow almost debonair. Bizarrely, I catch a glimpse of myself in a gilded mirror: a headless, traumatized figure in gore-rimmed torn pajamas, drink in hand, floating the lamest of bons mots at a crowd of swank, grotesquely ignorant party-goers — in a warm, sumptuous paradise of a room, amid ornate carpets and polished things gleaming in lamplight.

The metaphor is so calamitously apt to my life, so cruel, I almost sob with sputtering laughter at myself.

Outside, thunder trembles in the distance. Raindrops patter. Later there's a drunken variation of blindman's bluff. I lurch about, the numb center of attention, hands thrust out in front of me. Masked women squeal out of my way, and collide with one another in fits of merriment. The men watch, drink flushed, rubbing their jaws. Suddenly a flash quivers, an epic blast of thunder jolts the floor. All the lights go out. In the hubbub the woman who retrieved me seizes my hand. She pulls me through a door.

She hurries us stumbling up a pitch-black staircase, into a room. She closes the door, and throws herself onto a bed. Lightning pulses over us from the window. I sway there in dim panic. I feel terror, that my true state will now be revealed.

"No, don't," she insists in a whisper, still in her feathered gold mask. "Don't take off your costume. Hurry!"

I kneel onto the bed.

"God," she murmurs, as she grapples with her gown. She pulls me to her. "Oh god yes" she blurts, over the clang of the bedsprings. I feel her hands shockingly fumbling about on my shoulders, savoring my monstrousness. She cries out brutishly.

Then we lie on the dark blankets, with the lightning

flickering through the window. Squeals and laughter drift up through the floor from below.

The woman groans low and happy in her throat. "Now it's time, I feel, that you told me every little bit of your secret," she murmurs, nuzzling. She gives a sweet, slurry titter.

I can't speak. I lie there in gruesome distress, hearing the pelting of the rain. After a while, another sound joins in: snoring. Gingerly I raise myself in stages, to sneak away.

"Where are you going?" she demands groggily. Her warm, elegant hand fastens on my pajama sleeve.

In the morning I stammer out my entire doleful, appalling dream-history to her.

She listens aghast, contemplating me in disbelief. Her glossy finery is scattered by the bed; the wispy trash of green feathers litters her pillow. Suddenly, in a frenzy, she banishes me from the house.

Her revulsion rains down on me as I stumble out into the daylight. A flying golden cage comes crashing down on my heels. Big black rats burst out of it. They've all had their snouts chopped off, like sausage ends.

One slipper on a foot, the other in my hand, I go hopping away, a frantic headless man on a strange road in a countryside, pursued by a seething mass of squealing, pain-maddened vermin.

3.

I'm on a train. I ride the rails furtively, like a hobo. I'm trying to reach a pawnshop I've heard about, at a cemetery. They might have heads. It's a goods train I'm on. I'm in one of the boxcars near the back. I keep to the shadows, hands clasped around my knees in the loose hay. My travelling companions are the downtrodden, down-on-their-luck. I think of the phrase, "moths of the road."

To dissemble, I wear a bundle of rags balled up on my shoulders.

The train rocks and trundles along. Its whistle blast calls out to the night. The sound and sensation stab me with poignancy. The grade of the track turns steep. The train labors and climbs, then awkwardly halts, hissing. My hobo companions wantonly slide the door open to let the night in, even though company guards might be prowling. I hear gasps around me, like my own. We're on a hilltop. The gargantuan pale, glittering moon hangs right over the train, so big it resembles an iceberg we had drifted against in a little rowboat. The arc above us spreads out fields shiny like silverplate, blotched in places by torturous craters. A still, stolid splendor radiates.

The train takes on water from a clanking black silhouette of machinery, and wheezes. From our tilting boxcar the hobos gaze up at the immense silent bulk suspended blazing over us.

"Did the train ever go up to the moon?" I whisper, to no one in particular, deep in moon shadow.

"It used to," grunts a fellow next to me. "But that's a long time ago. . . ." Moonlight glorifies the side of his shaggy head, the grimy rim of his ear.

The train unhooks, and lurches again on its way. The hobos press into the door, straining to peer back as the great moon slides acre by glowing acre over the crest of the hill. The moonlight washes faintly and more faintly over upturned faces. The trundling of the rails fills the car.

Quite innocently, I stir up ill will by softly blurting, on a gust of pathos, that the moon is mine.

This is greeted by hoots of derision, curses at my grandiosity. One of the disheveled bunch, a cripple, insists provocatively that the moon is in fact *his*. The other hobos egg him on. He looks around for me with his grizzled chin thrust up, primed for a dispute. I withdraw further into the shadows. I huddle there, overcome by the preposterous squalor of what I've come to. Blearily I rock along, waiting to reach the pawnshop.

A game of cards starts up in the hay. I resist joining in, knowing they'll try to do me out of my bundle of rags. "And then I'll have nothing to pawn," I think desperately. I find myself playing anyway. Out of precaution I take my bundle down and keep it pressed against me as I sit. A couple of hobos stare openly at my calamity. The others glance up, then return to the melodrama of the cards.

I lose. The cripple cheats blatantly, clumsily. I protest, clasping my bundle, determined not to surrender it. The cripple squirms about on his knees, fumbling red and black cards out of his stunted sleeve. He works himself into a defensive lather. Sputtering, he accuses *me* of being the cheater. We lurch to our feet. The other hobos scramble up around us. The car turns lurid, airless with the prospect of violence. I smell the cripple's wretched stench as he rasps at me. It sickens me. The phrase "brawling with a cripple" harrows me like a caption for my degradation. I hear the hobos taunt and goad, closing in. The cripple brandishes his one intact fist and paws with his boots. His wrath makes him bugeyed, foam lipped. I clutch my bundle with all my cornered might — and then all at once, I twist about, and

bolt through, struggling, jarred by their fists on my pajamaed shoulders. I leap out the car door.

The night wind tears my bundle away. I scream, and
flounder. I land with a stunning jolt.

I stagger slowly up. The train blasts a long whistle as it
clangs away from me into the distance. Its black silhouette
curves by degrees back toward the moon, which hangs now
in the night sky like a tarnished silver globe.

I turn in a doddering half circle, and confront the night
forest, empty-handed, headless.

"But how am I going to find the pawnshop?" I hear my
voice faintly, plaintively, demanding. . . .

I kneel by the side of a rocky pool amid the moonlit
stones and bracken and stark tree trunks. I am utterly lost
in the world. An almost luxuriant, breathless sense of disaster grips me. I pinch myself and pinch myself in haggard,
plodding frenzy to wake up, until my flesh feels ravaged by
hornets.

But it won't help; it never will, I know. I hear myself
moaning in anguish.

My reflection sways in the water below me. I linger over
it in demented fascination. A gruesome Narcissus mirrors
me, clad in flannels for the coziness of bed . . . but lost instead in the wilderness of himself.

"I'm lost in the wilderness of myself. . . ." I bleat. "I've
lost my head . . . I've lost my mind that was in it. . . ."

In the water my hands play about over my shoulders,
over the grisly collar with its inconceivable injury. A jaded
and distracted fixedness settles onto things. The moon sits
at the edge of the pool and pours its sickly luster on my
hands as they wander over myself, slowly more and more

frenzied and caressing. I cry out brokenly, in turmoil and disgust and despair.

The dumb beasts of the night forest peer out at the din. They watch me in silence from all around: the leopard, the raccoon, the blinking owl, the anteater. I throw myself full-length onto the ground and wail at the top of my lungs from the depths of desolation and self-pity.

Then all at once I stop.

I raise myself. Another sound intrudes on the night. It's laughter. I heave around sluggishly.

A bear sits on a log. He holds his plump tummy in his paws and shakes his wide snout, and jostles with laughter. He has on a bright yellow-striped vest. His fur is brown, and he is generally round and even cuddly looking.

I am confounded — and groggily outraged. "Why are you laughing?" I demand, in a cracking voice.

"Because it's so funny!" the bear replies, his brow crinkling over his big shiny brown eyes.

"What's so funny?" I want to know.

"You, of course," the bear says. "You look like you're wearing a *flapjack!*" He waves a paw in a version of "too much" and dabs his eyes with the back of the other paw. "What're you having, a nightmare?" he hoots. " 'No head! No head!' " he mocks, wagging his own from side to side.

I am thunderstruck. "But I *am* having a nightmare! — You lamebrained, insolent —" I rasp.

All at once I realize his eyes are in fact buttons.

I swarm to my feet, my hopelessness sputtering wildly into fury.

"You're not a real bear," I erupt. "You're stuffed! You're a *toy!* How dare you patronize me, you —"

I rush him and throw my arms around him at the vest.

I wrench him up on his toes, shaking and squeezing with all my tattered rage. Our moonlit tableau is vaguely reminiscent of Hercules and the lion in the wilderness. Except the bear is relatively light, and soft furred, and bats at me meekly. And I wear pajamas, and show nothing above the neck.

"Ow! Ow!" the bear gasps. "You're hurting me!"

"Say you're sorry!" I growl, squeezing with a vengeance. I can feel and hear the squishing of his wood-shaving and cotton-bolting innards. "Take back 'flapjack'!" I snarl.

"I'm — sorry — about 'flapjack' —" he bleats, struggling for breath enough to say the words. "Ow! *Ow!*"

All at once his big button eyes burst from his head and shoot off into the bracken. I let go, jolted out of my passion by this graphic development. We lurch apart.

The bear huddles bent over at his plump waist in pain. His crumpled merry vest hangs down. He presses about over his snout with his paws.

"I can't see! I can't see!" he puffs. "You hurt me so! Ow, ow!"

"I'll find your eyes, I'm sorry," I try to reassure him, panting. I turn around, shamed at my ludicrous, berserk bullying. I start to comb dismally over the moonlit wasteground. The bear whimpers behind me.

"Here you are," I announce after a while, still breathing hard. "I'll keep searching until I find the other one. I'm sorry," I add again. "I guess I'm just pretty beside myself. Under the circumstances."

The bear takes the button and presses it back to his head. It won't stay unaided. He keeps it in place with his paw, as if it were a sort of dainty monocle.

"Why are you so angry and tormented?" he says to me. "It's *scary*."

"*Isn't it obvious?*" I inform him. I feel myself straining to keep raw temper from running amok again. "I happen to be stuck in a dream! I can't wake up! Can you understand?" I demand. "I've been *decapitated*, I can't seem —"

"You know what?" the bear interrupts, his paw still by his furry cheek. "You really should try to make a conscious effort to calm down. You can, you know, if you truly want to. It would make you feel a lot better, I'm sure."

I don't reply. I quiver from the labor of keeping control of myself in the face of such pronouncements.

"I was about to have a picnic," the bear goes on, "here in the pretty moonlight. You're welcome to join me. If you promise not to lose your temper," he adds.

I grunt. In penance and for abject egregious want of company, I trudge back as directed from a tree stump with the bear's picnic basket. We smooth a space and spread the tartan blanket on the stony ground. The bear brings out a pot of jam from the basket's checkered depths. He eats from it, clanking with his big spoon, after first dabbing a glob on his button eye as an adhesive.

I sit in bleak agitation on a corner of the cheery blanket. I whimper, exhausted, and rock.

"It's too bad you can't taste any of this," says the bear. "But you don't have to be so miserable. Look at me," he declares, scraping up a last sweet spoonful and clearing it with a curl of his tongue. "I'm almost blind, thanks to you. But I can still find pleasure in all this wonder above us." He indicates the naked night sky with a sweep of his spoon. I don't respond.

The bear hums to himself as he puts the jar aside and

maneuvers in the basket and produces a ukulele. A song, he suggests, will cheer me up. He strums. Slowly he begins to croon a tuneless kindergarten jingle. The jam around his button eye glistens oily and dark like a wound. I twist about in anguish, in excruciation at the horrors with which my grotesque unwaking imagination has visited me.

"Come on, join in," cries the bear, strumming away among the stones and bracken. "Jesus god —!" I blurt. I turn away, cringing, struggling to master myself. "Come on," the bear encourages. I shudder. All at once, the bear stops.

"You know what?" he announces. "You are really a rude and troubled person! Can't you see beyond your own personal woes? Let me tell you, however humble it may be," he informs me, "any art is a great aid and comfort. If you won't sing," he declares, "why don't you take a stab at making up a story? Go on; try. I'll be happy to listen."

I don't move a muscle for a long, apocalyptic second. A scene plays before me: in which I suddenly flail around, as if heaved that way by an internal geyser. "A story?" I seethe, maddened by the ad hominem of the irony. "What kind of *story*?" "There's no reason you raise your voice," the bear says, looking frightened.

"Answer me, I'm a writer!" I shout in my scene. Fury gushes through me like a ruptured artery. I seize the ukulele from the bear's paws. "What kind of story should I make up?" I scream, brandishing the little instrument in the night air like a club. "Please — help!" the bear protests. "Help!" He scrambles up frantically, making a shambles of the picnic blanket. "Answer me!" I howl. I lunge, and smash the ukulele on the ground, on the jar, on the blanket. The tinny crunch of thin wood and the jouncing of torn strings sends up a demented tinkling. The bear squeals. He huffs off into the bracken, squealing and yelping. I lurch off-balance to my feet. I swing the ukulele parts in the air above my shoulders, and they clink and clank and whir like the mechanical representation of an unsprung mind. I rant uncontrollably. The bear in his vest hops up and down from the distance of the tree stump, in an agony of terror and distress. "*What kind of story?*" I keep roaring, into the stony wilderness. "*I'm a writer! Tell me — what kind of story?*" High above, the tin pan moon tilts on its cockeyed axis. . . .

. . . . This scene erupts before me like the final spastic struggle of a condemned man. An ashen tremor sways me in my pajamas, and then drifts away.

"A story . . ." my voice echoes aloud. It's a small, flat voice, thin and empty, like a scrap of night wind. "What kind of story?" it wonders.

"You don't have to speak so softly!" protests the bear, there on our blanket. "Why, any kind you want," he encourages. "Whatever you like, you can make up a story about anything — anything at all!" He looks at me in a kindly, one-eyed way. "Your nice pajamas," he suggests, "you could make up a fine story about them." He laughs. "Or about me!" he cries. He coos, suddenly delighted and abashed. "I've always wanted to be in a story!" he confesses.

There's silence. "All right . . ." I hear myself whisper. A frail, inert cackle goes up, in salute to where my dreams have brought me. I quiver. The bear lays his unharmed ukulele down and wiggles around to get settled. He lifts his big grinning brown face upward in eager anticipation. "Go ahead, I'm ready," he announces. "But speak up! I said, I'm ready," he repeats, after several seconds. "Go on. But speak up!"

"Once — once upon a time —" I begin. My whisper veers and trembles. "There was a bear — in a striped vest — who went on a picnic. With his headless new friend — in pajamas —" The bear giggles, and nods gleefully. His chipped button eye twinkles in the desolate moonlight.

The halting drone of my fable drifts away from our tartan picnic blanket, out into the wilderness, out into the harsh, scarred acres.

"See how this helps you forget all your troubles?" the bear enthuses after a while, hearing the sputters of my cracked, madman's cackle.

Talk

TALK

"So you're not married?"

"No, I'm not."

"Never have been?"

"Of course not."

"I'm sorry, why 'Of course not'? Are you perhaps the type who, how may I say . . . prefers other company than women's?"

"No, no, please. But what sort of life can I offer a woman to share?"

"Oh, come now. Granted you live a bit like a romantic vagabond —"

"Excuse me: 'refugee,' you mean! I live like a refugee — caught in the turmoil of war. An internal war, for that matter! A man always in a ditch. Forever coming and going in ditches!"

"Well all right, if you — but even in such predicaments, be honest, one can find a partner. If one tries."

"Perhaps. . . . But then I've developed, you see, certain habits of solitariness. Of intimate independence. Set in my woeful ways . . . and my poverty. Lack of funds, money anguish: not the stuff for wooing."

"Now I'm sorry, but you sound like an old threadbare bachelor!"

"Do I? But then a bachelor who yearns for the domestic!"

"A quandary. . . ."

"An unhappy bachelor, with the moods of a whining child. An infantile, even demented, man-child. Forever seething at slights, forever muttering at the world and fortune for their bad manners."

"I see — I —"

"A grumbling loser, who hides away in his daydreams! Yes, and who's addicted what's more to dismal vices — to seedy consolations of the lowest sort! Hours and hours squandered behind despondently drawn shades! *Rubbed* away, *tossed* away! Do you follow me?"

"My god, please, there's no need —"

"To shame myself so? To expose my self-loathing, my shadow-eyed squalor, my gross insipid distress?"

"Please — listen — I mean, now I have a sense — you know, of your — your difficulties. I mean, why you haven't — settled down — and such — I'm sorry — Listen, I'm afraid I have to be going now, I've just remembered —"

"Nonsense, you can't go —"

"No — please, you'll tear the fabric! —"

"So then sit! Sit again. Come, there, have another, what were you drinking? I'd treat you, but I'm a little short, as always! Yes, you've got me talking now, I want to tell you everything, all about myself! How responsibilities frighten me — oh, do they ever! — and how these greying hairs on my head chill me with foreboding, with whispers of decay, of extinction. And of course — of course! — my calamities with women. Oh you'll cringe when you hear them, I promise you! Yes, you'll scream at me to leave off! 'So you're not married?' Oh it makes me laugh! A 'vagabond,' you call me! 'A romantic vagabond'!

"Come along then, travel with me, lose yourself in my disastrous fancies, fabrications, whatever. As I so like to do — as I have been doing all along, even just now! Here gabbing away to you. . . .

"Whatever it is you are."

THE SECOND SHACK

The phone rings. It's an old man, an eccentric type, an inventor. I did a job for him once. It's a couple of years since I've heard his voice. How did he know I happened to be passing through again, I demand. He didn't, he tells me. He just tried the number, out of despair.

He needs to see me, he says. He won't explain. He sounds distraught. He hangs up. I put down the receiver very slowly. I turn grimly back into the room, rubbing my temple. I curse softly, ominously, bitterly.

His place is a ramshackle cottage way out in the countryside. I get there in early afternoon the next day. I climb out of my car, grimacing in displeasure. The old guy comes through the screen door to the head of his run-down porch steps. He looks haggard, beside himself. He starts to jabber as I walk up, but then he just sinks into a dilapidated rocking chair. He wheezes brokenly about a bottle. I squint at him, blinking. I turn away and go slowly into the cottage. It's as crammed and jumbled as ever. The primly painted door to the lab stands out almost grotesquely amid the rusty squalor of the turbines and wiring and grimy glass spheres. The sight of the door sends a flare of pain through me. I grind my teeth at it. I push through into the kitchen and reach up to the top of a cabinet and bring down a bottle. I work loose the least unclean glass from the pile of things in the sink, and come back onto the porch.

I watch distastefully as he guzzles off the whole portion of what I've poured. He holds out the empty glass for more. I pull it away from him. I stare at him hard, waiting. He tries to grin shamefacedly behind the cracked thicknesses of his eyeglasses. He squirms in his chair. He looks older, graphically frailer. He twists himself and turns up open hands at the ends of thin, stiff, overapologetic arms. He promised, he blurts, he knows that, but he did something very stupid. Even after all that happened, he — My curse shuts him off in midsentence. I make a fist and press the palm side to my forehead, my eyes shut. I flap at him roughly to continue. He sputters on, almost in tears, conniving, about how he *knows* he shouldn't have, *knows* all the horrors of last time. But he thought — his voice starts to rise to that cracked, screwy pitch — finally he *understood* what went wrong before, he was sure he could do it properly now, he'd make *adjustments*, it would foster only *happiness . . . joy*! It would be the supreme achievement of science, *humanitarianism* — it would challenge — it would *challenge*, he squawks, the very name of God himself, and all the — I snarl at him viciously to shut up. I stand glaring down at him for long uninterrupted seconds. He cowers fraily in his chair.

I turn and lean against a scabrous fence post. I stare out at the wan disorder of the weeds and overgrowth. He snuffles away behind me. Without looking around I ask him how it got loose this time. He works to clear his throat, making bleating noises. Everything going wonderfully, he whimpers, its disposition was a joy to behold. But then a week ago, changes started to come over it. All of a sudden its mood would shift, it would moan and sing to itself in a fumbling way. Or it would become hostile, and break little things. Or it would just sit groaning and weeping and rocking back and forth. I listen to all this with my hand clamping my forehead. I have to shut my eyes again. The old man grew concerned at these ominous signs, the windows were barred but he took to putting an extra lock on the lab door before he went to bed. But he's old, he wheezes. Yesterday evening, when he unlocked the lab door to bring it dinner, it just surprised him, knocked him aside, and ran off into the night.

I hear his rocking chair creaking. He coughs and struggles to clear his throat. He needs the bottle again. I don't respond. There's silence. In a constrained, self-pitying whine he assures me how sorry he is to be turning to me. After all that happened..., he says. After his promise! But I'm the only person — "What happened before will never happen again," I inform him, my interruption tight voiced, low, lethal. "I am going to make sure, this time. *Forever.*"

I walk heavily down the steps and back toward the car, hearing his protests and pleadings behind me. But the slam of the car door and the noise of the motor starting up drown him out. I put the car in gear.

I go slowly along the dirt road through the deep woods. The latening afternoon light sits ponderous and lethargic among the shade trees and the engorged trellises of the vines. There's no sign of it at the crumbled mill site on the creek, where I'd first come upon it those couple of years ago. Nor farther on a few miles, at what's left of the first shack. I plod around the mossy ruin of planks and wall-paper, disbelieving, my face a stony mask of distress at find-

ing myself there once more. My breath comes short and laboring.

But I never really thought to find it at these places. I
climb back slowly into the car, and head on some miles
more, and then turn off ineluctably onto the weedy ruts of
a half-hidden carters' lane, toward the ridge, and, on the
other side of it, the destination of the second shack . . .
where a traveller dreamed a dream, once, of stopping. The
car lumbers and yaws, making its way on the last of the flat
terrain. And then all at once, it jostles to a halt.

The figure of a lone woman is sitting on an oil drum in
the early twilight, among the blackberry bushes. I stare
through the windshield without moving. The old man has
provided it with a different drab frock this time around, but
otherwise it's still as voluptuously barelimbed and barefoot
as the first time I saw it. It gazes back at me with mild fixedness through its makeshift, incongruous spectacles, over a
cupped hand of berries. I reach over fumbling into the glove
compartment and close my fingers on what delayed my de-
parture in the morning. I feel the dazed, agitated storming
of my heart. I get out. I go very slowly around to the front
of the car, and stop, panting, and lean a hip against the big,
warm grill, an arm stiffly behind me. The twilight woods
are utterly still around us, as if locked in motionlessness at
the very beginning of the world. It looks up at me, its
cupped hand lowered, its weak, beautiful eyes unnaturally
large and dark in the spectacles. It tilts its lavish auburn,
leaf-tangled head. The little tab for electrogenesis shows
under an ear.

"Hello," it says, in its strange soft low voice. It smiles
quietly, its pink-crafted, luscious mouth parted slightly to
show berry-darkened teeth. "I know you," it informs me

softly. It pronounces my nickname. I shut my eyes at the sound. When I open them, tears stream glistening down its rosy-tinted, smiling cheeks. "I have missed you so," it declares solemnly. "This time we'll stay together for more than two weeks, won't we? I won't be bad anymore, like I was last time." It raises a glorious, rounded, stitch-scored arm and points toward the ridge, and what lies beyond — like the herald angel of a darkly damaged, alternative paradise. A tide of passion and stabbing wounded pathos swamps me. "Nothing like that — is going to happen — ever again," I manage to get out, my words choked and thick. I jerk my hand into the open, and point, trembling. It looks back at me. "What is that?" it asks unsurely. It extends the blackberries toward me in a gesture of uncertain reciprocity. My gripping hand wanders back and forth across its target. "Monster!" I cry out punitively, at all the unholy, fabricated voluptuousness, tormenting, tormented. There's a dreadful pause. It starts to speak. "*Monster!* —" I shriek. The gun roars. Its catastrophic echo lashes away into the folds of the ridge, into the whole dimming immensity of the twilit world.

I lurch sideways, and go staggering around the car through the smoke, and throw open the door and collapse onto the seat. I drop the gun to the floor. I sit hunched over, my shoulders, my stiff-fingered hands twitching and quaking spastically, my face a contortion of noiseless anguish, of helpless, nodding despair. After a while, there's a soft, loony laugh in the open door beside me. "You shouldn't make such a terrible noise at the sky," the low, strange voice rebukes me intimately. "You could scare away the moon like that! Then what would we have," it asks, "to look at, when we go walking at night?"

And a soft, warm hand, moist from blackberries, presses itself slowly to my neck, and once again strokes it, clumsily and so tenderly, like a big, heartbreaking child.

Until I drive away.

Sacrifice

SACRIFICE

I'm becalmed, in an ancient place. Every morning at dawn, every twilight, I go down to the foot of the rocky cove and stare out past the empty masts of the boats at the inert sea, dark green and still all the way to the horizon. I mutter to myself and turn and survey a moment the coarse-shrubbed hillsides, the squat frame of the temple, where the smoke of devotion and supplication now rises continuously. I swing my cloak around me and make my way back up through the other watchers and mutterers, to the whitewashed cluster of rude houses, one of which I use as mine.

I doze away the heat of the day, brooding on my circumstances as I lounge on the sleeping pallet. Every so often I uncover my wound and probe it with the tip of a finger and grunt again. I roll on my side and stare out the deep-silled window at the blinding listless blue, and the dark green horizon, beyond which lies an island, one that I'm helpless to reach from here.

At first starlight, the girl comes to fill the lamp and cook my meal and tend me. In the light of the oily wick and reflected planets, she changes the dressing on my wound with uncertain, solicitous care. We consider the troubled flesh together, she gazing with wary fascination, myself with impatient disapproval. She binds me carefully as she can. She had never encountered a miraculous wound before, and I've had to explain to her its nature, how it will heal only by the hand of those who caused it. "But what if you never find them?" the girl wonders, her smooth young brow creasing. "Or it ends badly?" She looks agitated. I raise my finger to my lips and she gives a soft cry, seeing what's in my eyes. I bring her down with me to the pillows.

Afterward, when we've eaten, I recline on an elbow. I stare out through the window at the empty fanfare of the stars and masts. The girl sings to me, accompanying herself on the instrument that hangs on the wall. Her voice is modest, clear. She sings about the thyme that flowers by the stream, and a young girl's dreams of love. I turn my head and smile at her quietly. I touch at my wound. "What does your father have to say today?" I ask. She stops. She shakes her head. "Tell me," I persist. "He says the rituals aren't doing any good," she replies. "He says all the men will lose their livelihood if this goes on much longer. He says terrible, ugly things — about sacrifice," the girl exclaims, troubled. "But how can they blame this calm on you and your —" Her voice trails away as she says the word. I gaze at her. I don't answer. I smile again, somberly, half to myself. "You're very lovely, and very young," I think. I turn back toward the window, rubbing my chin with a knuckle, full of my thoughts.

I know what lies ahead. A week passes. Another arrives. I go down in the airless dawns, then again in the silence of twilight. The masts are immobile. Each time the crowd draws a little closer on my path back. I hear the mutterings echo. Things are spoken out loud; finally, shouted.

I come back to my door stonily in the ebbing light. I can't delay any longer what has to be done. The girl's entrance interrupts my brooding over my wound. She's startled by my look. She's brought a gift in her basket, to show how she's missed me these past several days, when her father made her stay away. I push myself to get it over with. Like a coward, I do it when she's bent away from me reaching into the basket. She cries out in wounded anguish, and twists around, recoiling. I repeat the phrases, trembling at their violence. She moans and throws her young head from side to side, and suddenly droops as if slaughtered to the floor. The gift shatters beside her. I step around to the door. My hand grips my pain where it flares.

I clamber down with stiff strides to the moonlit water. I rouse the drunken, snoring oaf I have as crew, and pummel him to haul up the canvas. I stand wincing at the tiller, peering off at the horizon with tears hot on my cheeks. A sailor's breeze erupts, tearing at my cloak.

CABIN

As dusk presses in, I chance on a cabin. I break into it and spend the night. I sleep badly, disturbed by dreams. At the first sign of dawn I give up trying to rest, and groggily take up my rucksack and get back onto the trail.

I'm in broken country, a distorted kind of landscape of bogland and insect-scourged hills. The air is damp, even with the sun up. The sun climbs and broods over the rank, wilting forest. By midmorning I'm overcome with a gross drowsiness. I force my way off the trail into the undergrowth and lie down in as dry a spot as I can find, and put my head on the rucksack and pull my hat over my face.

I gasp, waking. A hand shakes my shoulder. A figure crouches over me, another stands behind: local constables. "Get up," orders the standing, mustached one, addressing me in their lingo. I sit, blinking. "What is this about?" I murmur. "Eh?" comes the reply. I repeat my question in their speech. "Get up, get up," says the mustached one, obviously senior, coming forward and helping his partner pull me to my feet. I protest, but wanly, knowing whom I'm dealing with. The junior one carries a pistol — old, but lethal nonetheless. We do the customary business with passport. The mustached one hands it back and responds to my repeated question by instructing me to come with them. "But why?" I demand, weighting my tone as much as caution permits. "I have business elsewhere." There has been a crime, I'm informed.

We trudge back along the path I came, the heavyset mustached one in front of me, the armed one following. I listen to their grunting, the squeak of their absurdly well polished boots. After sweating an hour of this, I flare up in complaint — "Where are we going, I told you I have business elsewhere!" — but the only response is a dark, warning look directed at me over an epauletted shoulder.

Eventually the cabin comes back into view. I see the door ajar and splintered from where I broke the old lock. I protest about the circumstances of the evening, that I took the cabin as abandoned. "I'll make full restitution for the damage to the door," I declare, wearily computing how much the bribe will have to be, how absurd and bombastic the protocols of authority hereabouts. "We are not concerned about a broken door," the fat constable with the mustache informs me. I regard him in confusion. The two of them lead me to the threshold. I look inside uncertainly, and I give out a hoarse gasp.

The crumpled figure of a girl lies in a corner of the cabin. Her head is twisted unnaturally, with a lurid bruise on her forehead. There are more bruises on her neck. Her eyes are wide, gaping at the cabin's low, moldering ceiling. "I don't know anything about this," I stammer. I'm shaking. "I spent the night here, I told you, but the cabin was dark, I saw nothing. I only had matches for light." I make an absurd, quaking gesture of lighting a match. I go on frantically. "I was just in that bunk," I protest. "I know nothing of this. I left right at dawn — even before." The mustached one stares at me phlegmatically. He asks for my rucksack. I open my mouth to argue, but I think the better of it.

Trembling, I take off the rucksack. He indicates the bunk. "Sit," he says.

The two of them squat outside the cabin door, going through my possessions. I watch them in dismay. My eye falls on the remains of matches by the bunk, and I pick them up hurriedly and cradle them in my hand, as corroboration of my account of the meagerness of illumination during my time here. I gaze over in horror at the dead girl. There is something piteously sorrowful about her, under the weight of gross brutality visited on her. The whole horrible business swamps me with an intimate, heartsore chaos.

The constables come back into the cabin. "What business is it, that you are on your way to conduct?" they demand. I stare up at them, unable to answer right away. "It's personal — personal business," I get out at last, fumbling with words. They blink at me and slowly turn their heads, and exchange a look. "I tell you I know nothing about this, I never saw anything, I've never seen this unfortunate woman before," I protest, my voice starting to break. I exhibit the two charred match remains uselessly to them. They regard me, frowning over my hand. I look over haplessly at the girl. I throw up my arms, shaking my head in despair from side to side. "I'm innocent," I bleat, in strange turmoil. "I know nothing about this!" But I make the mistake of telling them about the dreams I had, what I remember of them.

HERMITAGE

I betray a girl's romantic trust and decide it best to slip out of town. I pack my few things and make off once more for new locales in the mists of dawn.

But guilt casts its black shadow over me. I've shattered someone's heart, a heart I loved too, in my distracted fashion. I drift through a couple of towns, ill at ease, drinking with sullen intentness. One afternoon I read in a newspaper, now several days old, the crudely worded account of a death. I sit rigid in my chair.

I renounce the world and wander into the wilderness. I find the abandoned cave of a charcoal burner, and I take up a hermitage there. The odor of burned things and stone seems exactly fitting to my soul. I feel myself in a state of damnation. I brood on my life, which is not a life, I now understand, in the scathing clarity of my grief and remorse. Tears course down my cheeks as I catalogue my history of betrayals, abandonments, agitated neglect. What has love meant to me but affection triumphantly stolen? What achievements can I show but a knack of creeping away from complications, of slipping off in the midst of things, to search out new artificial beginnings. The cave wind blows through me, the breath of absence. An emptiness, like the uninhabited night all around, which sets its compass at me and swings over the blank pages of my book. Over waste, regret. Tears drip into my beard as I softly beg a wandering ghost, somewhere, to forgive me.

My mind goes. I light fires in the cave and rock the days away in the blinding smoke. My eyesight fades. The spirits in the stark woods around there notice, and take pity. They scare off the beasts that prowl in wait as I stumble down to the stream to draw my water. They channel the flooding rains away from my stony bed. They set a songbird in the bramble outside my threshold, to bring a cracked smile into my distraction.

Then they go too far, and dress up one of their company as a mock girl, and send her wandering near my cave to have our paths cross at twilight. They do this out of misbegotten kindness, but also because, being spirits, they have a taste for mischief. I fall desperately in love, as a madman will, though this ensnarer has a snout and tusks, and bright wild berries for eyes. I take her for my lost beloved returned to me, coarsened by the grave.

And so, I suppose, this is how I redress my sins. My crimes paid off in cruel absurdity. Smoke-blinded I sit by my fire, hugging tight to my enraptured heart the grotesque comfort of my solitude. I console her murmured sobs with protests of her beauty. I pledge my devotion, I stroke the rough hairs of her muzzle, whispering and clucking, while the sooty cave echoes around me with hoots and giggles.

MEMOIRS

I grow old and grim. I shut myself away in a room in a town somewhere by the sea, and set myself to finally writing my memoirs. No fancies anymore, no evasions, no fabrications. Just my bitter pen scratching the harsh accounting of where I've been, what I've done, how I see myself and the world.

This plain speaking, of course, is absolutely foreign to me. It doesn't come naturally at all. Mainly I gnaw my pen and groan and rip up the dumb pages into a litter of frustration. Late afternoons I glumly stalk along by the waves, hands buried behind my back, grinding my teeth in rumination. I cut an eccentric figure, with my bony ankles and flapping pants and carpet slippers, and a handkerchief tied around my head like an old woman. The local children like to trot along behind me, mocking. I wave them away irritably. I stop and turn around and curse them.

To grow old, I think, is bad enough. But to grow old and finally decide to spread your life's cards on the table and then to fumble the deck. That is God taking the joke a bit far.

But so it goes. I chew my pen, I crumple up days' worth of intimate commonplaces, I heave them into the corner, onto the banalities piled on banalities. This is my existential agony: my drivel. More and more I just sit on a bench

at the beach, with a stick to poke at the sand, and the handkerchief on my greying head while I brood on the one-note
symphony of the waves. One afternoon a brave little girl
comes close and stares at me quietly, and then asks me a
question about the handkerchief. A brief sociability flowers,
a few minutes long. The girl ends up with the handkerchief
smartly over her braids. But then her mother calls over,
sharply, and snatches the handkerchief off and leads her
away with a hard look over her shoulder at me and the character I present. I lean forward and stick my tongue out at
her, and hear the little girl's faint giggle of appreciation. I
jam away at the sand with my stick, grinning.

I tell this story to the bar girl at the wineshop, where I
put in, increasingly, on my way back to the stark labors of
my room and its paper mounting into rubbish. The girl
clucks her tongue in admiring approval of my grey-haired
mischief. After a fair amount more wine, she plucks my old
nose. She giggles at my jokes. I recite selections from my
desperate scribbling, and she hoots with laughter. I impro-
vise spur-of-the moment elaborations, flight-of-fancy self-
parodies. She roars. Gleeful, I grab her juicy wrist and lean
across the bar to snatch a kiss. She cries out, and slaps me.
She curses. She orders me out.

On this ugly note, I abandon the evening. In fact I decide to abandon the whole confessional fiasco altogether,
weaving back to my room in my carpet slippers, hand to jaw.
And I do, I dump pen and paper and sandy handkerchief out
the window, and pack up and go back to the sort of writing
I know. To bits of lying and make-believe; very much like
this story, for instance.

TESTAMENT

Ilie dying in a remote backwater in a distant part of the country. I have them put out a makeshift bed under the shabby tree in the courtyard of where I've fetched up. It's hot, the off-season, although given the lack of charms of the region, no season is prime.

The daughter of the place leaves her cleaning and dim-witted bookkeeping chores to tend me in my sickbed. She is young and docile, plump in the favored local manner, if hardly a beauty wasting away in these forlorn parts. Dutifully she tamps my sickly feverish brow and passes me my water cup and regroups my sweat-damp pillows. She brings with her an intimate ponderous aroma, of flesh and life.

One afternoon I grab her hand as it's on me. I whisper to her, in a feeble voice, for a dying man's last honor. To be allowed to touch her just a moment under her skirt. She stares at me. I try to pull her closer. "Please," I hiss. "Just a moment. For a dying man." She wrenches free and runs sobbing in a cloud of dust toward the crude front door of the place.

The proprietor appears over my head in a fury. He is burly and sweating, and waves a fist above me that's like the haunch of a boar. I cringe hollow-eyed in my pillows, plead-ing apologies. I manage to placate him with some of the loot in my bag, the loot that will eventually have killed me. For more of it, and more abject promises, I get the daughter to resume her ministrations. She performs these in the most wary, desultory manner possible, an aloof scowl on her wide, round face as she stiffly maintains a distance a yard off.

I pay out the long, dismal hours brooding on my end in this dirty backwater courtyard — on the calamity and waste that have comprised my life. Flies gnaw at me as I cough and sweat and stare out at nothing across the dust flats, the dust-colored cactuses, the rubble of hills on the horizon. Coarse and washed out in the twilight. Perfunctory. Then, darker; dark. Blank. I try liquor, but can't tolerate it.

I feel my life draining off like dirty rainfall in a gutter, and a feverish passion comes over me, to put down a confession.

I'm too weak to write myself. I ask the daughter if she has notebook and pencil, and for more of the loot again, she sits on an upturned box behind my head and scratches along slowly while I disgorge myself, panting, of my memories and sorrows. Then I'm done for the day, and she hurries off inside while I slump back, resounding like an overstruck bell with meditations, with regrets. Tears stain my haggard, drifting sleep — and a crude intimation of grace, a sense of an accounting of my dim childhood . . . silly hopes of young-man days . . . wayward, wasted maturity. My callous ineptnesses at love and home. And dismal fortune. . . .

At last, my voice frayed with emotion, I call for the pages to be read back to me, by my transcribing angel. The house cur slumps in the dust nearby, tearing stolidly at the side of his head with a paw after fleas. But there's only sweat and silence. I slap limply at a fly. "Read, please," I insist hoarsely, eyes shut fast in preparation for my reckoning.

"But I can't read —" the daughter's voice blurts. "I can't write —"

I stare stricken into the glaring, grey sky. The daughter giggles chaotically, the notebook tumbles to the ground as she runs crying out toward the door. The dog leaps to its feet and cowers, barking at my flapping leg.

The proprietor emerges and stands with his fists on his hips, gazing toward me as his daughter, hand to her mouth, points from behind him, to where in the desolation and anguish of my last hours I hang halfway out of my bed, clawing in the dust at the notebook, at its doodles, its gibberish.

Tissue

TISSUE

I eat some odd food at a street stall. Up in my discount room, I don't feel so well. I twist in the grubby sheets, sweating and whimpering, in and out of sleep, my mouth pink from stomach soother. At some point in the night, a harsh thirst seizes me.

I find myself out in the corridor, paper cup in hand, poking along groaning for a water dispenser. The hallway has been changed, I note blearily in the dim light. But its cement floor and faded maroon paint seem somehow familiar, in an intimate and disturbing way. Shambling along, I realize with a pang that I'm in one of the houses I lived in as a child. I smell the telltale odor of its hallways, faintly gritty and clammy and oily. "Have they turned it into a hotel?" I wonder plaintively, grimacing. I slow to work loose a queasy burp. Then I halt.

Two small shadowy figures, a thin woman and stout man, are in profile outside a doorway. I watch them argue with someone barring the threshold. Their luggage slumps beside them. The sound of their garbled elderly voices — mainly the woman's — sends a spasm gusting deep through me.

They're my parents, long carried away from me by the brutal tide of the years, by the final sundering of life's fraying rope. "How poignant and wincingly thematic," I think, realizing what's going on overall: "That it should take the

side effects of a bad meal, for me to see them after I don't
know how long." I cry out. I drop the paper cup. I shuffle toward them.

Our reunion is strangely perfunctory, low-keyed.
They're frailer than I remember them, seedier, as if beaten
down by the unrelenting seasons of travel — like the in-
sides of luggage that's no longer protected en route. They're
much distracted. The hotel manager there on the threshold is evicting them from their room, for lack of payment
or some such embarrassment. The shabby euphemism
"embarrassment" seems to rise from them like an odor. I
grimace, rubbing my stomach. The arguing garbles on. I
offer to settle the bill, but I'm ignored. The hotel manager
won't yield. I manage to persuade them to come to my
room.

Finally we start down the corridor in ragtag fashion. But
their patched-up luggage proves awkward to maneuver
down the narrow hall. My father squawks. To my agitation
we just stop halfway along, like cattle stuck midstream. "But
I want to show you something very important!" I protest,
sweat dripping, the whole underlying issue of our encounter
now stark to me. I lurch on ahead to my room and fish
through my own bags, grunting in discomfort. I hurry back
out to them. Panting, I exhibit the swaddling of tissue paper.

"Remember this?" I whisper hoarsely. My voice is tight
with emotion. Slowly, I uncover the reliquary scrap of
gilded tin.

My parents peer, looking blank. They stare up at me.

"You don't remember?" I protest. I'm trembling. They
look at each other. They shake their heads, taken aback by
my emotion.

I blurt out the history of the item, fighting back tears.

"Oh, yes," says my mother. She assembles a brief, coop-erative smile. "How nice, how nice," she says. "You see, this means so much to me," I inform her softly. "I think of it as a kind of holy relic," I add, with a little pink tremulous grin, my voice almost cracking. I allude to the extremes I've gone for retrieval. My whispers sound inane in my ears.

There's an awkward, off-kilter pause.

"You did all that for a chunk of some toy?" says my father, scowling in his stained green felt hat. His voice wobbles in gruff disbelief. "My god, you're a grown man," he says.

I stare at him. I stare at my mother. I blink. I don't know what to say. After all this time, I realize, this is what it comes to: Nothing to say. I swallow. I shrug. I grunt, out of mul-tiple reasons.

I help them tug their luggage by stages back down the hall, to the stairs. They're finding another hotel. It doesn't come up that I join them. "I hope you're not wearing lip rouge these days," says my mother, groping along. "And tell me, it takes a bad dream from food poisoning for you to see us?" I don't answer, fighting with the tangle of bags going down the stairs, my treasure stuffed into the pocket of my T-shirt. Below lies the living room from yet another address of childhood. The hotel manager scowls from the sideboard fruit bowl as we strain through the front hall, the screen door, down the wide porch steps.

Finally we and our load are on the sidewalk. A street-lamp hangs its dim moon over us, by a big childhood shade tree. My father sweats down his unshaven beard, my mother reties her seedy souvenir-shop scarf; I pant and gasp beside them. My father's suddenly frenzied, flapping arm, to hail a taxi here on this residential street, is like a terrible flag

shooting up a pole — the streaming banner of all the hy-
perbolic anxiety of our family's travelling history. I sway at
the sight, the blow of memories. It occurs to me further my
parents might not have cab fare. It's too harrowing to ask. A
taxi somehow appears. There's a hue and a cry loading the
wretched bags.

"Now you — take care of yourself," my mother announces, patting my chest lightly in good-bye next to the
tissue-y lump in my pocket. My father mutters something
from the open cab door. The moment resounds with my parents' distraction, their grimy preoccupation with the burdens of where they're off to next. The taxi draws away from
the house, grinding gears, no hands waving from the dark
windows. Then it's gone.

I stand there in the night street, motionless. There's a
long, inert silence. I blink down at my pocket. My stomach
twinges. I squirm. Suddenly, from the depths of my being,
I shriek. I wrench out the packed tissue. With every fiber of
pent-up fury, I rush forward, and in anguished rage I hurl
the papery artifact in the direction of the vanished cab, its
departed fares. My flimsy lodestone travels a few feet in
midair, then appropriately stalls and shivers toward the
ground. I lunge for it and flail with my fists — like a man
gone berserk to bludgeon the dying moth that chewed up
every item of his clothing. When the renounced charm in
its swaddling reaches the ground, I stamp on it, flattening
it into trash, grinding it out of my night back into the brute
earth. I rant obscenely, sputtering, spraying the air pink. I
grab my gut and roar on tiptoes, like a madman.

It goes on like this in the street from my childhood, even
after a door opens, and an officious voice calls out. Outraged,
it demands to know where exactly I think I am.

Music

MUSIC

After the plane crash, I decide it's high time I give up my wandering life once and for all, and settle down. Where I am in tropical mountains seems as good a spot as any.

I set about shopping for a suitable partner for domestic life. After so many years banging around alone, I'm not much of a hand at these matters. I make the mistake of bringing up my air disaster. "But I thought there weren't any survivors," my dates murmur, looking up in confusion from forks poised over local, *flan*-style desserts. There's a little awkward pause. I clear my throat. "Actually, I'm not a survivor, as such," I admit, with a sheepish laugh. I waggle my chin in good-humored self-deprecation. "I'm one of the so-called 'tragic victims,'" I declare. There's another pause, of ashen silence. This is followed by a scream, or a curse and sign of the cross; or in one case, a threat to call the police.

I realize, under the circumstances, it's best I kept my mouth shut. This produces results. I manage to nurture a budding relationship with a lively young woman who, appropriately, runs the local travel bureau. She likes to dye her hair a different color each week — as a form of cosmetic travel, she notes, with a grin! This sort of drollery is dear to my heart. I begin to indulge hopes. Then one afternoon, as dusk is settling, I stand foolishly by the window, flipping through brochures while she gets ready to close up for the day. Suddenly from behind me I hear a strangled gasp. I turn around, and am informed, in strained, horror-hushed tones, that she can literally see right through me.

I'm forced to make a clean breast of things, long before planned. "My god, go away — leave me be!" I'm hissed at, by the voice of someone crouched down in hiding behind a desk. I can just make out the top bob of a brand-new champagne-blond dye job. "Get out of my shop — and my life!" I'm ordered.

The next morning a nervous priest appears at my door, in the ruins of the former pensione where I'm squatting, and announces that if I make any further attempt to consort with a certain one of his flock, I will find myself in the gravest trouble imaginable! He mutters something about "You unquiet ones," and waves a big black crucifix at me, and scurries in retreat down the broken stairs.

I am so disheartened, I just sit in the rubble of my room with the door locked, immobile for hours on end. Bleakly I stare off through the window cracks at the minor sun-washed plaza beyond, and out beyond that, the ill-fated peaks and crags raising their glories against the blue sky. Perhaps, I despair . . . perhaps I've simply waited too long to cultivate the domestic. And so my fruits are this sequence of catastrophes in both modes, physical and emotional. The bitter harvest of delay. "I mean, who wants a spook for a mate?" I ask myself. I close my eyes at the answer.

I find myself brooding away afternoons out at the poky cemetery where they've got us and our remains. I prod some daisies into the mud by the grave marker, and clean up the wilted litter scattered by the mountain wind from the day before. The wind blows its lonesome sigh in my ears, and

I'm faced with the bleak truth, that this is the only tune probably I'll now hear: the music of loneliness.

And yet. . . .

And yet, somehow, the innate spark of hope that inspires the heart of life — of being among the living — comes to my aid. I take my morbid self in hand. I give it a shake. "Now who do you expect to meet, up here in a graveyard?" I demand internally. But then I realize: "Why, just the right person — if you keep your eyes open. Someone with a passing acquaintance with the Departed."

I start monitoring the bereaved comings and goings around me. Not only at this particular sanctuary of those passed on, but at the drowsy little town's other one, there behind the rough stone of its venerable basilica. Happily a yawning priest presides here. And here it is, not too much later, where my eye falls across the jumble of memorial rows, onto an appealing, round-armed and thirtyish graveside visitor — an early widow, perhaps, judging by the clutch of memorial posies in her smartly gloved hands.

Just what I'm after. I drift closer. From behind a droopy cherub on his pedestal, I spy the name on the gravestone she attends; and the jowly, middle-aged and mustached visage inset in its commemorative photo medallion. My breath quickens. I trail her auburn-haired, dusky-necked form out to the gate. I watch her walk off, the tight black warmth of her dress catching the mountain sun like the pelt of a seal. I turn away, and make straight for the shade of a café, where I raise a fuss until I'm supplied the use of the grimy slim local phone book. A thrill shivers through me: I find one lone entry for the name I reconnoitered in the graveyard. It bears a "Mrs." in front of it; and an equally heavenly

suffix: "Music Teacher." I sway on air back to my cup of bitter chocolate at a corner table.

That very afternoon I arrange my first lesson.

And so begins my late-schooled courtship. I whisper not
a word about airplanes, accidents. I avoid dusk-hour ap-
pointments. I apply myself to my instruction, which turns
out to be on the accordion, an instrument that stands in for
the piano, alas now too dear for my teacher's widowed circumstances. So her crowded, cheerful parlor resounds to my
straining, sluggish fingerings of polkas and waltzes and
sprightly military marches. Tunes from worlds and oceans
away. Unexpectedly, I find myself drawing compliments for
a native musical sense; which makes me want to blush, if I
could, with posthumous childish pride.

While my teacher imperiously pries my hands about
with her soft hands over the buttons, I venture a tidbit or
two from the glamour of my wanderings. Over a pot of tea
afterward, she talks a little in turn about the late man of the
house, lost in his prime two years before when his car ran
off a mountainside to avoid a cat, and plunged into the town
reservoir. No drinking water for a week, she recalls
somberly, dropping another brown lump of sugar in her
cup. The cat turned out to be a crude toy, set in the road as
a prank by local teenagers no doubt. No culprit was ever
found.

The ill-served victim looks down at us from his foggy
photo portrait over the armchair. He was in the small-scale
import business, apparently with no appreciation of culture
whatsoever. Brought her up here when she was very young.
But he worked hard, was decent, and paid for their home.
And for her beloved piano. Which she had to sell — alas,
alas! — and replace with the humble accordion.

The accordion leans against the side of the hearth like a boxed, soft-gleaming bellows. The widow sighs.

"Up in these mountains, it hasn't been easy, finding someone who appreciates culture . . . music," she declares, and she gives a haughty twitch of her pretty nose. I smile at this. I go further, and grin, intimately. She blinks at me. Then quietly — intimately — she grins back. A note chimes in the parlor between us, struck by the heart. Her eyes flicker up and down over me just a moment, noting something. I glance down at myself. I gulp, jarring my teacup.

I can make out the cushion I'm sitting on, through my wavering cotton trousers! I stare horrified out the window at the advancing twilight: a ghost in the grip of dread. "I have to be going —" I blurt, struggling up, flinching in distress against the oncoming screams, the curses, the prospects in ruins. The widow sighs again, in a tone of regret. "And here I was about to invite you to stay for dinner," she announces airily. And she leans back and raises her joined hands to her lips, and regards me over them, her eyebrows slightly lifted in amusement, and her eyes narrowed.

A woman unalarmed by the undead.

Our romance begins in earnest that evening, after a domestic serenade of claypot chicken and the ubiquitous local chocolate and corn and *flan* variation, and most of a bottle of fizzy acrid wine from her holiday stock. At last we lie together in the brocaded sheets of her bed, she honey brown and plump and naked, groaning softly in the crook of my grey arm. At last I have a tender someone to spill it all out to, the final moments of the flight, the nightmarish veering chaos of the cabin as the pilot struggled — the shrieks, the strange windy silence afterward, the desolate —

Suddenly she presses her fingers into her ears and winces. "Enough!" she cries. "Let's talk about happy things!"

I'm shocked.

"All right," I tell her, swallowing, flustered by her blunt, unkind vehemence. "All right, I'll — I'll tell you some more about my travels," I offer. "No, not that either!" she protests. "You've talked and talked about them enough already! They're all so gloomy!"

I am entirely taken aback now, by such a peremptory dismissal of the trophies of a lifetime. "Well then what should I talk about?" I murmur tightly at the lacy shadows around us, in insulted distress.

"Kisses!" my amorous widow whispers. "And only sweet, intimate things!"

And she means it. As our passion blooms into odd, loving domesticity, I am shown an astonishing new world — here cracked up for good in the mountains — where my far-flung wanderings and trials are simply of no interest. "Why would I want to hear," she announces, "all about the troubles a lonely, rootless man got himself into, in the course of a strange and mainly wasted life?" Which puts some things in a nutshell, I have to admit.

She sees me as little as possible in public, because of the scandal of my condition. She insists also I dye my hair, so as to look as if among the living. And she dusts me with powder puffs from her cosmetic case, to make me presentable, those times when we ramble the main cobblestone plaza of an evening.

I continue my lessons under her supervision. (In truth I'm her only pupil.) Her parlor swells with my wheezy approximations of tangos, of barcaroles. This is how I do my travelling now — musically, as well as via the guidebook

I'm tinkering away at in the privacy of the proper boarding house to which she's had me move. The guidebook contemplates the region's cemeteries, which after all were the birthplace for our propitious meeting ... were the venue where I resisted the plaintive drone of the wind, and kept faith in my search for a harmony.

One sour note strikes into my happy requiem. Periodically the dead husband shows up. He misses her cooking, it seems! The widow feels an obligation not to turn him away, out of gratitude for past domestic generosities. And from a vestige of marital decency, though his nattering on and on about his current living conditions, she exclaims, drives her to distraction. No intimacies pass between them, I'm assured. Even so she can't bring herself to tell him just yet about the new dead man in her life, for all sorts of arcane reasons. This gets my goat, in no small way.

But what's a ghost to do in these matters — and one determined what's more, regardless how late, to renounce his days of roaming solo, and learn the art of being two? Just accede, he must; and strive for composure, and wisdom. I draw some solace from the harsh dismissals the other must be subjected to, whenever he tries wanly to bring up what life's like on the other side.

So the couple of days every few months he's around, I busy myself off touring mountainside cemeteries, and tidying my notes. I make a point of keeping my spirits up, while I amble past the headstones. When the breeze tries to play its sad song in my ears, I whistle my accordion tunes over it, and practice my button fingering.

And soon enough I can return to the hearth I've won the right to haunt — a dyed-haired specter reunited with his posthumously adulterous Mrs. The parlor seems clammy to me at first, from the watery interloper's visit. But we take up our instrument once more, we resume our lessons, my musical widow and me, and things regain their hospitable warmth soon enough.